CABALA

Published by Dog Horn Publishing
45 Monk Ings, Birstall, Batley WF17 9HU

doghornpublishing.com / sales@doghornpublishing.com

Cover images from:
Cabala, Speculum Arts et Naturae in Alchymia by Stephen Michelspacher (1654)

Editor: Adam Lowe
Typesetting: Adam Lowe
Assistant editors: Matt Read and Gemma Rutter

Additional thanks: Wes Brown, R. L. Royle and The Rusty Knuckle (R.I.P.).

In 2009, five writers based in Yorkshire and Greater Manchester undertook a ten-week programme of masterclasses run by Dog Horn Publishing and hosted by Borders Leeds. This anthology is a result of that process.

'Touch Sensitive' previously published by Serpent's Tail and 'Half Life' previously published by Social Disease, both in 2007. 'Girl Absorbed' previously published in 2009.

Contents

Half Life

by Richard Evans

Centropolis™ sprawls outwards in perfect symmetry, its intricate streets coated with afternoon rain evaporating into evening sun. I stand on a curved ledge atop a financial edifice floating a kilometre above the surface, buffeted by harsh winds. No matter that this is summer, it is forever cold up here and my thin clothes afford little protection. The golden sun sinks into the horizon, drawn down through wisps of violet cloud by an insurmountable force. Commuters traverse the chasms between iridescent buildings through a matrix of elevated tubes, for the streets are the dangerous province of the poor and the desperate.

"Take it easy, Quaid." The PsiCop creeps along the ledge, her movements insect-like in her strict black uniform. A visor covers her eyes, keeping me guessing as to her intentions. "Name's Vasquez and I'm here to help."

I look at her pale hands, uncertain whether the flesh is genuine.

"Whatever it is that's hurting, we can change it." She shouts over the billowing wind.

"I've seen too much change."

She sits a meter away. "How 'bout we just talk then?"

Cold gusts slice into my lean form. "I'm three hundred years old, and yet these bones do not wither." I touch my shaven head with a youthful hand. "This construct is a sensate prison for an ancient mind."

"What are you telling me?"

"The original flesh was weak . . . so they made this body for me. But now, all those that I loved are long gone."

She taps her elaborate headgear and the visor dissolves, revealing exquis-ite brown eyes. Her voice softens, she whispers on the wind. "You aren't the only one."

I look down at the shimmering streets and then at Vasquez. She offers a tentative hand and I tremble as the next world beckons.

Everybody's Got Talent

by Jodie Daber

The audience are naked. Thick leather straps restrain them and their open lash wounds ooze. They are savage with exhaustion, their hands clapped to meat. On the stage a woman tries to force a scrabbling pangolin to suckle at her rouged and leaking nipple. The pangolin coils itself stubbornly around her arm and she looks up at the Judges' Box and sobs. The audience scream off, off, their abraded voices like a flock of terrible birds.

In the Judges' Box Suckling sits, hooded and in heaven as a roasted, thumb-sized songbird leaks its juices over his tongue. He is just about to bear down on the bird, to crack its back against his soft palate and lick away its breast, when he is nudged by Mrs Isinglass and inadvertently swallows it whole. He pounds his buzzer without removing his hood and the woman on stage is condemned.

Rubber-suited Production Assistants stride across the boards, grinding diamonds between their gleaming teeth. The pangolin scuttles wisely away. They pick the woman up, a leg and a wing, and toss her to their colleagues in the aisles. An empty chair is found. The woman's sobbing grows louder as they strip her, but she doesn't scream until they buckle her in.

Backstage the holding pens stretch for miles, chicken-wire cages with concrete floors and a chewy reek of greasepaint and sweat. Inside them the contestants limber up, la their scales, fix their feathers or sit and shake and sob. A pair of gilded twins fill each other's mouths with honey. A chunky middle-aged couple in matching sequinned cocktail frocks lug a paddling pool brewing with grubs. Several somethings sort of akin to sloths hang from the quivering outstretched arms of an otherwise naked man. Everyone has their number tattooed in the palm of their hand.

Assistants stalk the pens in wipe-clean suits and rubber boots with heels that look like hooves. They carry clipboards edged with razorblades and the necessary tools on their belts. They cherry pick the choice contestants, separate the beautiful and the wrecked, the stars and the scum, the fattest and the strangest and the ones who will win. They will perform at prime time, when the paying audience comes.

A small boy sits with his side pressed to the chicken wire and his knees drawn up to his chest, trying to make himself even smaller than he is. His long coat bulges considerably at the back. He received the summons three days ago and his parents panicked. Neither of them had ever been called and out of terror and a cringing kind of hope they convinced themselves he would be safe, too. When the envelope came, hand-delivered by a grinning Assistant, his mother had collapsed.

The boy could not sing or dance or vomit on demand, he was neither winsome nor imposing; he was a pale and rather clammy child with no discernable talent at all. His mother had taken to her bed and his father had taken to the bottle and somewhere in their fevers they had a terrible idea. His father went out in the boat for a very long time while his mother force-fed him rum.

A muffled offstage call of "Next!" heralds a tumbling troupe of eunuchs, bald and bejewelled and naked below the waist. They squat and shit, singing jumbled falsetto arias as like hulking babies playing with clay they sculpt their waste into swans. Isinglass pauses for effect as she dislodges the dwarf latched like a lamprey in between her legs. Below her the besmeared eunuchs pant for her verdict. She stubs out her cigar on the dwarf's scabby head and smiles a little like a jackal. "People like you," she says, "are what this competition is all about."

When the eunuchs have been led away and the stage perfunctorily swabbed, a tiny old lady stands in the spotlight and swallows a fly. The audience bellow their derision. She reaches into her smart wicker hamper, raises her hand —a spider, big as her palm. She swallows it, gimlet-eyed. The audience pause. They think they know what's coming. A golden cage drops down from the flies and a blue-plumed bird cocks its head.

In the Holding Pens, the man with the sloth-like things loses it. For hour after hour he has stood in silence but all of a sudden he is screaming get them off me get them off me and clawing at the creatures on his arms. The contestants closest to him take a quick step back but the ones behind them press closer, straining to watch him falling apart. Within a minute, the Assistants are through the crowd and upon him. One tries to pull an animal off the gibbering man, leaps back when she sees the way his skin has grown over its claws. The man is dragged away through tunnels to a seat in the audience, buckled in appendages and all.

The old woman holds up the velvet collar and makes the little bell tinkle. Her belly is hugely distended underneath her housecoat. The audience whoop themselves silly as from the wings comes a worried whining. In the Judges' Box Mrs Isinglass doodles elaborate cocks in the margins of her scorecard.

The boy stares at the number in the palm of his hand. 4,357,776. The Assistant with the fanciest clipboard calls out "4,357,765!" The number is starting to scab. He scratches it because he knows he shouldn't, scratches harder until his palm is wet. His father is waiting in the Friends & Family Suite, a cold warehouse with nowhere to sit. Later on, an Assistant will tell him the verdict. They have made plans for all the outcomes. His father made him repeat them over and over again. He looks up. Through the chicken wire, an Assistant is staring at him.

"You should have gone for a smaller breed," says Mrs Isinglass, as the old woman and the retriever are carried away, each looking as grim as the other. "Next!" The glamorous couple pull on their paddling pool and slip off their heels. To their own strained twitterings they dance a stationary tango ankle-deep in wriggling bodies. The audience seems pleased. They finish their act unimpeded. "You are the best example of this kind of act I have seen all day," Mrs Isinglass says, and the couple are escorted offstage by Assistants. It is a short walk to the Vans but it is a long drive to Boot Camp and the glory of Round Two.

Now the boxes fill with the great and the good, the rakes and the bloods and the gals-about-town, dignitaries and millionaires, celebrities and the propped-up husks of previous winners. They nibble on thyme-infused tallow cones, the hot, crisp ears of hares, breast milk parfaits and silver punnets of wasps. Jewelled beetles crawl on their lapels, larks rustle clipped wings in teetering nests of hair, the heavy scents of lead and lavender clag the air. They are the paying guests and they expect the best.

And so the pick of the bunch are paraded onstage, the best of the best and the absolute worst, the talented and the deluded, the damaged and the great. A woad-daubed woman inflates chickens with a trumpet, the spatter reaching to the fifth row and further. The honeyed twins loose swarms of bees from the most unexpected of places. A beautiful woman panics and gnaws her fingers to the bone. A lithe young lovely performs a human ouroboros. The paying audience largely ignore them, looking instead to themselves and their rivals. Mrs Isinglass checks her watch.

Then the boy stumbles on stage as though pushed, clutching his thin coat closed. He staggers centre stage and pauses, suspended for a second by the noise and the lights and the wall of stinking heat. Then he thinks of his father and swallows, lets fall his coat, drops prone on the splintery boards. Clumsily stitched along the little boy's spine, the dorsal fin of some huge fish flops. With his arms by his sides and his mouth open round, he writhes.

On the other side of Isinglass, Gentle Fudge slumps, blood beneath her fingernails and a rolled note up her nose. She racks up another line on her vast, blue-veined breast and when she can't quite reach it she inflates herself a little more. Isinglass pokes her in the nipple and she looks down at the little boy, scenting parents' tears.

"Ooooh, yummy!" she says, in a voice like rancid butter, "I want it! I want it! Put it in a basket and give it to me!"

The talent parades on, cold magicians with leashed assistants, Trojan cats and wilding clowns, man-made centaurs and stigmatic virgins and the Great De-Gloving Machine. In the Friends and Family Suite the supporters of the successful clap each other on the back and the rest slink home to begin the long and lonely years. Somewhere beneath the theatre in a dressing room littered with needles and filth, an oversized picnic basket gives off a whiff of boy-sweat and fish as a puddle spreads beneath the wicker. The audience bay and strain and slap their bloody paws together and from the box above, the gods rain down their slops.

The Milky Bar Kid is Dead

by A.J. Kirby

The Milky Bar Kid is dead. He bit the Californ-I-A dust. Popped yon popsicle clogs. Met his candybar maker.

The Milky Bar Kid is dead. They'll hover the dang flags at half-mast for the goddamn halfling. They'll call a national day of mourning for the slapped-arse face mini-cowboy, gosh darn it. Childrens everywhere will wonder where their next milky bar will come from, because they'll no longer be *on him*. Haw haw.

The Milky Bar Kid is dead and we'll all be forced to wear blue and white checkered shirts in commemoration of his image. We'll don shrunken Stetsons and bind our own feet so we can cram them into childrens's size spurred boots. We'll have to slam on they milk-bottle Milky Bar specsses just so's we can show we are strong an' tough like him.

The Milky Bar Kid is dead and I killt him.

Yippe-ki-ay motherfucker.

There, I said it. And, oh, I know what you're thinkin'; I must be some sick psycho with a soup-bowl hatred of all things chocolatey and shiiiit. Or there must have been summpin from mah growin'-up days—some uncomfortable memory of a whip-talkin' stranger enticing me onto his bronco with a bagful of milky bars—which warped me forever. But it's not like that at all. Sure I killt him, but I reckon he was god-dang already dead.

I wipe the thick white foam from mah pint of Guinness off mah handle-bar 'tache. Wonder when the terrible news is going to hit the wires. They got the rolling twenty-four hour news service on the idiot-box behind the bar here. About five ticker-tapes scroll across the screen. At the moment, said breaking news ain't really news at all, but when they find out about the untimely demise of ol' Milky, the screen will explode with excitement.

'. . . dead . . . The Milky Bar Kid is . . . ' the tickers will say. They tend to sound like Yoda if you happen to catch 'em mid sentence.

The red ticker which moves diagonally across the screen like a slash from Zorro's sword, or the Peruvian national soccerball team's shirt, will suddenly start churning out block capital warnings. The blinkin' sun yellow strand at the bottom —the one that usually contains the dollah news—will start flashing like a dag-gang beacon. The newsreader will have to try to stick his city-boy orangey suede through all of these virtual prison bars just so's he can get a look in.

I wonder how the news will hit with the good folk in the bar. Wonder whether they will break down. This here barkeep, Chico, looks as though he on the edge of taking a rope to his ol' neck every day anyway, what'll he be like when he learns our gosh-darn kindergartenhood hero has gone overboard? He's always had that Mehican shuffly-feet misery about him. You can see it by his peekers; never any hope in they peekers. An' they saddlebags which ride along unnerneath his peekers; this man ain't slept since godknowswhen.

An' how's ol' Maggie, the sour-faced trick-turner, going to cope when she hears that El Kiddo Milky-Barro has been skittled? She's a weepy kinda wo-man at the best of times. Not that a man could ever say she's had a best of times. But. But she looks as though the slightest dang thing could push her over the edge into raving loony and I wouldn't want to be the trick caught under all that weight if she did turn coyote.

But at the moment, I'm the only one that knows. Part of me revels in the knowledge, yessiree, but another part of me feels as guilty as sin. Is guilt a sin? I cain't remember mah Seven Deadlies these days, but I'm pretty dang sure that murder is one of them. Back then, when they wrote 'em, they called it summpin else. Iss all about brandin' an' marketin' these days, ain't it?

This here town could do with a bit of the old marketin'. The place is like one-a-them ghost towns nowadays. The streets are mostly deserted, like. Every-one's off somewhere else, either down they labs, or queueing for a loan so's they can register for they labs. But River's Bar is comfortable enough. I've been comin' in here ever since I came up to Cally, an' by now, mah ass has kinda settled into the grooves on the barstool. Sometimes, a man finds hisself noddin' off on said stool, despite the six-shooter digging into hiss leg.

River's Bar is like kinda el-typicallo Wild West saloon type. Has them doors a-swingin' when a fellah walks in, not that many fellahs walk in these days, but yer know what I mean. Has a pianner over in the corner and card tables out back. It's a place where you drain the hoss right where you sit and nobody but nobody eyes a batlid cus there's sawdust on the floor and the place plain stinks anyway. It's the right kinda place to sit and wait out the fuckin' cavalry. It's the right kinda place for a miseryguts like me; a man that had it all, I s'spose, but pissed it all up the wall by being a forgetful so-and-so.

It was forgetidness what did it, your honour. I gosh dang took my eye off the ball, only for a moment like, but it was enough. I got guilt on me, riding me down like all they rootin', tootin' hosses. Try to think of summmpin else. Try to think of summmpin else.

'Hey, Chico,' I call, 'fetch me a Diablo to go with this black stuff.'

Chico barely even looks up. He's a-starin' at a stain on the woodchip bar, mayhap hopin' that it'll just disappear if he stares at it long enough with they acid-misery peekers of his.

'Cheeks?'

Wearily, like a hoss that has been rid all through the darkness hours with no el watero, he raises his head. Kinda shuffles over to where I'm sat, proppin' up said bar.

'Yezz?' he asks.

'Drop o' Diablo to keep the devil from the door,' I says. 'Sniffter o' bourbon for your old chum Cotton-Eye Ed.'

Chico just nods, dully, and reaches up for a dusty bottle. No label on the bottles here. It's prolly juss reconstituted piss wrung out from the sawdust.

'Good day today, Cheeks?' I asks, for conversation's sake.

Chico free-pours, bottom lip all jutted-out like a ten-year old's. Like the Milky Bar Kid would have done if everyone went took all his bars one day. Chico cain't remember a good day. He deposits the clunky, lip-stick marked glass in front o' me and doesn't bother askin' to be paid ferrit. You pays later. You always pays later in this joint. This life.

Mah eyes whip back to the telly, where summpin is happenin'. For a moment, I's afeart that iss gonna be the news that I juss know will come upon us all. What will come to pass will come to pass. But I reckons iss juss the adverts.

Ad break: A science dick is on, prattlin' on about summpin or other. I reckon it might be summpin to do with New Life, so's I better pay attention.

'Oi, Cheeks; ratchet up the noise on the idiot box, wills yer?'

Chico is slow to obey, but obey he does, grabbing the biggest remote a man ever seen and clickin' a few buttons on it before he finds the right one. Iss like he never seen it before.

' . . . and with our new packages from the Time's Not Up Corporation, you can rest assured that you will be awoken from your sleep feeling refreshed, revitalised, rejuvenated . . . '

'Retarded,' I snapped. Nobody in the bar paid me no mind.

The idiot in his idiot box carried on: 'Way back in June 1965, the Time's Not Up Corporation, made a promise. We said we would take one *friend* for freezing for free.' And here, said idiot held up one stiff little finger, like as we didn't know what *one* was. 'And now's the time to make good on this promise. Only now, we're offering an even better deal. The first one *thousand* good folk that contact us will get frozen for free.

'You'll sleep in luxury, and be woken up in some happier future with absolutely no side effects whatsoever. So, if you're tired of the lack of current opportunities . . . If you think the grass might well be greener . . . If you believe that *you can be better* . . . Then a New Life from the Time's Not Up Corporation is your one-way ticket!

'Jesus said "bring me your sick, your elderly, your infirm"! Come unto us and we can keep you alive, ready for a time when you *can* be saved! Our friends, simply call this freephone number and we'll take you through all the details.'

I store the number in mah suede for future reference. Fiddle with a dime that's just magically appeared from mah back burner.

'And remember,' concludes the science dick, 'our references are the very, very best.'

Images of Walt Disney. An' Bing Crosby. An' John Wayne. An' all the gosh darn All-American heroes filled the screen. All of 'em dead. Or should I say frozen, ready for repatriation. Some reckoned it was the new government in wait-ing, should they finally be shook awake. *Some reckoned.* Iss all well and good this cryogenic-freezing lark but what happens if some idiot like me stumbles in and fucks it all up for them? They don't say none of that on the advert. They do have the small print o' course, read out bullet-fast at the end o' the infomercial so's nobody not on the old wack can unnerstan' it, but iss there, juss in case the root-in', tootin' trades description honchos are listenin' in.

There's loads of these freezin' companies about now. Iss like when ah was a youngster and they were sellin' off plots of land on the moon, the powers that be knew that they'd prolly never have to make good on their promises, and saw it as a way of makin' an easy buck. Nobody really expects to be woke up from the cryogenic freezin', and once they inside the freezin'chambers, they cain't exactly complain even if they ain't gonna get waked up. They offer up a few free-bies to the sick, or the mad or the half-dead. Dangle the carrot that life could be better for them in some desert-mirage future. Most have to pay though. Most have to pay an' iss a big scam, most o' the time. An' as with all good scams there's good money in it. Good money for fellahs like me, even. Yeah, even me dipped a toe in that partiklar water meself. But now's not the time to be thinkin' about mah mistakes, is it?

'Hey, hey, Cheeks?' I yell. 'Cheeks!'

'Uh-huh,' he sneers, all Clint Eastwood or whatever that Mehican cow-boy's called.

'Hey Cheeks, see that ad with the Bing Crosby on it and the Walt Disney?'

'Uh-huh.'

'Know the difference between the ol' Bing and the ol' Walt, d'yer?'

Chico looks non-plussed. Hell, he lookie-likie he never heard a joke in his whole goddamn life and that's the truth aymen.

So I goes: 'Bing sings, but Walt Disney.'

Chico looks e'en more confused now. Like he's been transported to some other dimension where no man speaks Mehican at all at all. It don't do me no fa-vours when a fellah don't even attempt to laugh at one o' my jokes. I return to my Guinness, which ain't going down so good and Chico returns to pretendin' to clean the glassis. Ol' Maggie, who'd looked a bit interested for a minute back there, when it looked as though the first person may laugh in this bar for nigh on twenny year, but now she returns to her own nasty-work. She's got her hand rammed right up her gingham skirt and I don't wanna know what the hellshes-doin'.

It's like that in here. Mind yer own business, if yer got a business that is. Most callers don't. No siree boss. Most fellahs that trundle on in here don't even have a hoss to tether outside. Most fellahs don't remember the good old days. But me an' Maggie-guts do. Me an' Maggie remember when Coughin' (or was it Coffin; I cain't remember) River used run this place an' it was jumpin'. The card games got up high prices, the jukey was allus playin' the best kinda songs. Milky Bar Kid ads were on the idiot box.

It ain't Chico's fault things have turned out this way. Not at all. When he came in, things was already on the downward slope. Just seems everythin' in life ain't as rosy as it used to be back when we all had that sunburn-sheen of youth on us. Back afore everythin' all went all so damn cynical. Milky Bar kiddo used be the symbol of all that was innocent, really. I mean, 'magine him on the idiot box now, huh? They'd make him take off them speccses for one, else he'd get em all smashed up. Or they'd give him corrective eye surgery down one them clinics out Western Boulevard. They'd probably make the kiddo a girl an' all. To boot. An' they wouldn't say he wus strong an' tough, they'd say he wus good at math or foreign languages or summpin, or that he was anti-war, or that he wus an interior designer.

But knowdin' how this dang country is now, knowdin' how maudlin we all get, an' how we all gotta show our grief in big black strokes just to show we alive, everyone'll go all out crazy like I says about the national day of mourning an' that. Even though they take piss outta him when they think he's alive. People wanna have they cake an' eat it. We cynical one day, but if summpin happens we wanna be able to behave juss like kids again and go mashin' our teeth and wailin' like there's no tomorrow. Thass why I'm worried what'll happen to me, once they find out what I did.

Dang. You can't smoke indoors in these parts. Not any more. So I got myself on the tobbacci-gum instead, but it ain't the same. Makes el Diablo taste like goddamn mouthwash. I'm fiddlin' for summpin with me fingers but cain't get a hold of anythin'. Maybe I should make a grab for Chico's idiot box remote and fiddle with that. Find another channel, maybe the rodeo one. But I won't do that. I 'm too . . .

Poor ol' Milky Bar kiddo. Poor ol' us. I'm startin' to feel all glum again now. The Milky Bar Kid is dead and right now, chief, it feels like I'm a-dancin' on his grave. I shouldn't be sitting in this here bar drinkarooin', I should be handin' mahself in at the sheriff's rancho, going down on bended knee and praying for leniency. But I cain't go down there cus when they find out, I'm going to look like a right bewildergoose, ain't I?

Thing is: the Milky Bar Kid ain't the only one I killed. There were others, countless others that I just let off the merry-go-round without a second thought. I gone killed allovum. Every last one that was ear-marked for that New Life thing. I pulled the plug. S'jus that with ol' Milky, that's the onny one I felt any kinda remorse with. Hence the ol' Guinnessaroo. Hence el Diablo.

I always was forgetful, chief. Ever since I can remember. An' I cain't re-member much. Some wiseacres might say that iss on account of all the shiiiit that I slurp down that big gullet o' mine, but. But I know that it started even before I started on the hard liquor. Started when I was younger an' shoulda known better. Juss couldn't be bothered, I suppose. Had other things goin' on in mah head, like uh whatever I happened to be thinkin' about at the time. Went about in what folk called a daze, so it's damn amazin' anyone trusted me with anything or maybe not. Mayhap they trusted me on account of the fact that I'd never turn snake on 'em cus I wouldn't remember none of what happened.

What was I thinkin' about? Oh yeah . . . Time to pay a visit. Time to drain the hoss. An' then I'll make a phone call. My last phone call.

Ahem. Sorry 'bout that. Guinness has a nasty way of goin' right through me. Better get on with what I was gonna tell yer about before iss too late. Here goes:

Fellahs that knows me round these parts know me as the kinda *unofficial* sheriff anyways, or so I'd like to think. Mah official title is Security Oper-A-tive. And as part of mah job I was to keep an eye on the Cryo-Unit underneath that there famous, or rather infamous ranch out in the hills. Got the job through this here bar, believe it or not. So, ma, what yer said about sittin' drinkin' all day long never doin' any man any good wasn't quite correctamundo, was it? If I hadn't ha been exactly where I wus now when them fellahs from the security corp came a— knockin' then I'd ha been juss lassooin' thin air like the rest o' the no-marks that are left round here, wouldn't I?

They signed me up then and there on the spot. No real contract or anythin', just a man's word. Some might have said I was stupid not findin' out more about these fellahs, but when they gave me a nice uniform an' the like, I knew I was onto a winner. They gave me a six-shooter an' all. To boot. A sleek, pistol-whippin' black number that kinda whispered the word *damage*.

Seems to me like they security goons were as desperate to employ little ol' me as I was to be employed, or at least to have some dollah in mah back-burner. The ways I see it is most people round here didn't wanna work. Not when they could go off an' get frozen an' wait for better times instead. Not when they could juss chill in the chiller for a while an' not even worry about anythin'. So these security men wus probably feelin' like they struck gold or summpin when they found me willin' an' able.

There wus two of them. Both big guys. Army grunts really, I suspects. They wus neither ovum wearin' 'taches, which made me a little wary, but you could see that they had that kinda outdoorsy feel to 'em. That outdoorsy thing always makes me trust a man better; like they know what life is an' how hard it can be. Anyways, it wus all surnames with them. All 'pleased to meetcha Drood' an' 'come with us now Drood'.

After I signed up, they led me out into the street—deserted as always —to this big gunmetal grey van thing that looked more like a ship or summpin. Slammed me in the back like I wus a prisoner. I couldn't see into the front of the van thing, but they kinda relayed their voices back on walkie-talkies or whatever an' they tellt me that I should get changed into my uniform right then an' there.

'Don't worry, we ain't watchin', Drood,' oneovum says.

'We ain't lookin' at yer pecker,' says the other. Like they a regular comedee team or summpin.

So I yanked off mah kecks an' mah shirt an' slipped into their uniform. I say slipped into it, but it wain't as easy as all that. Not with the van thing bumpin' an' bouncin' along the roads at some fair rate o' knots; barrellin' into the bends like a stock-car. But I managed it somehow an' soon started tryin' to look out the tinted back winnder.

We wus goin' high up into the hills. Cactis country. Coyote country. Ban-ditland. All big boulders sunbathin' an' the shimmerin' of yellowbrick petrol on the roads. In the distance, I seed what I think is the ranch we're going to. From here looked more like an amusement park. Big yellow slide things, a merry--go-round. Didn't really fit in with the kinda sepia tones everythin' else has slipped into round here.

We fair baked along inside, me and these security men. It was startin' to get agonizing. I felt like a kid, 'bout to ask *are we nearly there yet?*

'Hey fellahs,' I say, bangin' on the metal dividing wall that separates me from the front cab o' the van thing. 'Hey fellahs!'

Cracklin' on the innercom.

'Yeah, Drood; what is it?'

'Well . . . um . . . what we doin'?'

'We're off to see the wizard,' says oneov they jokers.

The wizard, I think; what they on about? Are they takin' me for a gad-dang fool, here?

'The wizard at the end of the yellowbrick road,' says the other on this fuckin' crazy-ass tag-team. 'At the end of the rainbow.'

I decided not to banter them up no more. Not until they stopped sound-in' like they acid-poppin' Beatles off Eng-ur-laind. So I carried on starin' out the winnder. The roads were bendy, like, so sometimes I could see the weird ranch risin' up in the distance; other times it wus over the other side an' it felt like I'd been imaginin' it all along. *At the end of the rainbow*, sheesh.

The van thing screeched to a halt. After a moment, the back doors slid open an' the twoovum are standin', arms folded, lookin' at me. Bothovum were drenched with sweat, like they been dunked in the waterin' hole on main street. Bothovum looked mean as fuck. Not wantin' to give 'em the satisfaction, cus I ain't got no, I jumped out the back of the van an' gave this silly salute thing like from the movies.

'All present an' correct, sirs,' I says.

'Aw, we ain't yer boss, Drood,' replied oneov they men. They were like clones, them fuckers. Or like them double-acts on stage where one's a puppet an' the other one has his hand up the other's ass. 'You'll meet the boss-man soon enough.'

He says it all menacin' like; as though he wus tryin' to scare me. Make me quiver in mah new boots.

'The boss don't like a lot of people around him,' says the other security clone. 'Not *grown-up* folk anyhup.'

And then they both gave me this shit-eatin' grin and said no more on the matter. But the way they were actin', I knew that there was summpin funny afoot.

'Come on,' they says, takin' me by the arm. 'Juss a little walk an' we'll reach the gates to the ranch.'

Juss a little walk, they says. *Juss a little walk!* By the time we reaches they gates, I was as sweaty as the pair ovem and I felt like pullin' off the top ov mah uniform-overalls.

The gates were kinda big an' old and like summpin from a filum about Eng-ur-laind. Through 'em, I could see more o' this rancho that I was apparently gonna be stationed in. Still looked more amusement park than any ranch I'd ever seen. Lots of weird statues linin' the driveway; all depicted one man that I half kinda recognised. Manicured trees like cartoon characters off the idiot box. Lurkin' off in the background was this low house like a football pitch bungalow, and further off than that were the slides an' the rollercoasties an' other things. The other things, I reckoned, might have been zoo enclosures. Certainly, when a man stopped to listen, he thought he could hear faraway tigers a-roarin' an' parrots a-parrotin'. Was like that place at the end of the *Citizen Kane* filum, in actual fact.

This figure came outta the bungalow thing wearin' what looked like a sheet over allovhim. He had a cowboy's kinda rhinestone walk, like his ass wus all jiggered from too much ridin' o' they hosses. Couldn't see any part of him but I knew who he was straight away off the idiot box, like. It was blazin' hot out there and all blurry above the tarmacadam but I knew who he was alright. Whisper it now, man . . . You knows who'd it gonna be dontcha?

'Iss Elvis,' I says.

CABALA

One of the security dicks nodded solemnly like he was the last cowboy off the whole dang herd.

'We workin' for Elvis?'

The boss gives this hip-swivel by way of response. Now I'm not sayin' that feller under the sheet *was* Elvis an' I'm not sayin' he wasn't. There was no way of tellin' really. Couldha just been oneothem lookylikeys, fed up on squirrel-burgers for year upon year. But the security dicks seemed to think that it was okay to keep on callin' the boss-man Elvis and that was fine by me. Ahm not one to question a direck order . . .

An' anyways that's how it started. Mr. Elvis was a-waitin' for us behind iss sheet but he never said nothing to me. Juss looked me up and down and kinda grunted. *Ahuhuh*. He kinda gave this ghostly salute to us all and then floated off somewhere else like he had no legs to speak of. Or like he was so fat now he had to have wheels affixed to his goddang legs.

I felt like sayin' all kindsathings to the man, but I wus all tongue-tied. Not that he wus a hero of mine, but when you see someone in the flesh, or under a sheet as the case may be, that you seen on the idiot box *so many* times before, it juss kinda hits you how fuckin' ordinary everythin' is, despite the fairground rides an' the white sheet. He wus juss a fat kid playin' hidey-seek for cryin' out loud.

After he'd moved off, I juss kinda stood about for a bit and waited until I got my orders off someone else. I mused about stuff, an' thought about how nice it would be for Chico to set up a stall sellin' ice-cold beer right here outside the gates. He'd get as many customers here as he did in the main street, for Christ's sake, an' e wouldn't have to pay any overheads, or keep ol' Maggie in gin.

Finally, one of the security men came up holding out this bullet-proof vest to me. I took it an' shoved myself into it, despite the heat.

'You're lucky,' said this security dick, checkin' with his mean eyes that el Wacko had well an' truly scarpered back into his funfair. 'Mostly Elvis don't come out to see the new recruits . . . Oh he used to, of course, but once all that shiiiiit started with him s'pposed be dead, well, he's stayed off the radar. He's what you might call a recluse these days, like that Howard Hughes.'

'Oh,' I says.

'So the King's alive?' I ask, all a-wondered.

The big security dick gave me a withering look, as though weighin' up how much to tell me. Well in for a dime, in for a dollah. 'You heard what happened to ol' Walt Disney?'

'Yeah?'

'Well, Elvis-baby's after doin' a Walt Disney. Freezin' hisself. Cry-oh-gen-i-cally. Already done it once, when it got, uh, bad.'

He wus spellin' it out like I couldn't unnerstan' English, like Chico, man. So I decided to play it professional like: 'What you be wantin' me to do?'

'You're to watch the freezin' chamber,' he says, an' wanders off.

The freezin' chamber was located unnerneath the Pirates of the Caribbean ride in Elvis's funfair, juss like Walt Disney's was said to be unnerneath that same ride in Disneyworld . . . or -land, a man never knows which is which between them two. Anyways, part of the fun—or what that ol' trickster Elvis thought was fun—about it was that a fellah had to actually walk the dang plank an' plunge into the waters in order to find the entrance to the damn lab-unit. Once in the water, you kinda had to swim unner the shit-ship an' fire in this code onto a keypad. Was like enterin' a submarine, lil ol' me supposes.

Inside, all wus dry. All wus a bit un-King like to tell the truth. No mad shit like outside, juss science. Bleepin' machines, whirrin' engines, hummin' 'lectri-city; many, many idiot-box screens showin' what was goin' on inside the countless pods which were arranged on the floor. Part of me wus a little shocked, or even worried when I saw some of the people—chillen actually—that Elvis had inside they pods.

River Phoenix, Michael Jackson, Macaulay Culkin, the little fellah off *Austin Powers,* The Milky Bar Kid, the one outta *The Goonies,* some kid outta oneov the new *Star Wars* filums. Loads and loads of 'em. So many that it wus like one of Chico's *Where are They Now?* quizzes back at River's Bar. All frozen, all Lost Boys. Thass what he calls them: Lost Boys.

My duties, such as they were, were to make sure that there wus no alarms off the pods. It wus a bit like ol' Homer Simpson in his power station, simply watchin' for flashin' lights. Couldn't have been easier. A machine couldha done it. CCTV couldha done it. Hell, e'en ol' Maggie from the bar couldha done it.

21

But it wus me that did it. An' you knows me. A fellah can get used to anythin'. But not boredom. An' that wus what it was like down there. Once yer got used to bein' amongst a waxwork museum of oldtime kiddo-celebs, yer kinda juss forgot all about it.

'All right, the Milky Bar Kid?' I'd always said when I signed into work. Never anyov the others. Juss him. Suppose I'd kinda grown to like the fact that he couldn't answer me back an' that. But summpin about the way he looked unner all that reinforced glass _did_ make him seem more alive than the rest ovum. Like there was still summpin there unnerneath that glazed, speccy expression of his.

After a while, I started to take in a few computer games an' such. A mini-fridge. An idiot box. Like Security Oper-A-tives everywhere, I made mahself at home in the place unnerneath the Pirates of the Caribbean ride. Only problem was the lack of the ol' 'lectricity. Sometimes, I'd be right in the middle of watchin' some key piece of plot from a _Columbo_ episode an' _slam,_ the idiot box would juss fizzle out into nothin'. Why, juss lass week I happened to be playin' _Perfect World_ when wouldncha know it, the power conked out again.

Well, 'nough is 'nough, I thought, an' before I really knew what I wus doin', I'd unplugged Macauley Culkin an' was back in the game. Suddenly, all this harsh wailin' came from Macauley's pod, like he was wakin' from the dead or summpin. I half jumped outta my skin an' I don't mind tellin' you that. I thought he wus gonna smash right outta that pod an' eat me alive . . . But then I realised it was the machine tellin' me that I'd fatally cut off the fellah's oxygen supply, an' for a moment I breathed a sigh of relief.

As soon as I realised the full situation, o' course, I was mortified. _I killt him, I killt him,_ I thought. I'll be sacked. I'll be taken to walk a real plank off a real shit-ship. I'll never drink at River's Bar again. Never really bothered thinkin' what mah thoughtlessness had done to ol' Macauley, mind, but them's the breaks mah friend.

So when ah went home that night, I wus sure I was gonna get woked up any minute by a brayin' at the door an' a clamourin' for blood. I was sure my god-dang time was up, yessiree. But nothin' of the sort happened. Thing was: the se-curity dick that followed me never noticed. He wus probably as forgetful as me. Hell, probably he'd killed a few ovum before hisself. Mayhap, the fellah from

Dozzee's Cartoon Club was already dead. Mayhap the chap from *Kid Kapers* had already popped hiss clogs.

So over the past week, I been quite lax to tell yer the truth. Neglectful of mah right and proper duties. Lazy. An' when I wanted that cold beer with mah pickled ham, I went right on an' pulled out the lifeline for Chubby Davis an' hardly had a second thought about it. The way I figured it, they people weren't really alive at all. They wus juss tricked into givin' up their lives to lie in these mad pod things so Elvis could watch them on his own idiot box to his heart's content. Nobody could wake up from cryogenic freezin'. Stone cold fact, or so it says on the innernet.

So I got even more lazy. Even more forgetful. Even more set in mah ways, like everyone that has a shift-job will tell you. Clock-in, clock-off, thass about all's you can remember. An' when yer wages are in, you canin't remember anythin' anyways as you're likely so dang drunk that you forget all about what really goes on unnerneath the Pirates of the Caribbean ride at the ranch in the hills.

But when I pulled the cord that linked to the Milky Bar Kid's pod, all that thinkin' changed. Cus ol' Milky did come up for air, juss for a moment. Was like he wus fightin' against all the Milky Bar snatchers from days of yore. Juss for a minute. He kinda craned hisself up a bit, turned his head to face me. Glared at me with his little screwed up halfling peekers. An' then he pointed with his ikkle bitty finger, direct at mah heart. Accusing. As he did so, he let out this great gaspy screech of childish anger an' then flopped down again. Dead.

He was definitely dead. Dang nailed-on. The machines, the heart-rate monitors an' that all told me. But his finger was still pointin' direct at me. He hadn't been like that before. An' even I would have noticed if one of the people in the pods suddenly changed position overnight. That wouldha been dang scary.

It was dang scary. An' so I skidaddled, back up through the water. Back up onto the pirate ship. Back past the merry-go-round and the water slides. Back past the football pitch bungalow. I kept mah head low as I passed the gloved fist and made the gates, finally. Only when I gunned the engine of the van thing did I hear that bloodcurdling *ahuhuhuh* shriek comin' from the house. Elvis. The King

So here I am, the killer of the Milky Bar Kid waitin' for this town's unique brand of justice to come a-knockin'. An' it will come soon, no doubt about it. It won't be the sheriff. Not now the dang wailin' has started up; carryin'-on through the dusty hills like nobody's business. Rattlin' the bottles on the shelves of River's Bar. Fair sends a shiver up a fellah's spine sittin' here an' juss waitin', but then I s'ppose I been waitin' here most my adult life for summpin to happen. Now summpin will happen soon 'nough. Sure, summpin will happen that'll take every kinda decision I ever had outta these paws o' mine.

Mayhap I'll die from a bullet, mayhap I won't. But whatever happens, I knows that them security dicks are on my tail, and in true Wild West style, they'll most likely invite me outside for a shoot-out. Out there by the old waterin' hole, by the wooden poles where a man can tie up his hoss. In full view o' the misty eyes of ol' River's Bar they want me to meet my end. An' they'll know that though I may be quicker on the draw than one o' them, I'll never beat the two ovum.

So thass why I'll ask 'em a question first, afore the shootin' starts. I'll ask 'em. I'll ask 'em whether they know that I already made that phone call. The Time's Not Up Corporation will be here soon too. Here to collect the latest of their friends that has won a free freezin'. Good job I made that call.

I don't know whether I was just imaginin' it about ol' the Milky Bar Kiddo. Mayhap he woke up an' mayhap he never did. But thinkin' back on that scary moment earlier in the day, I know that there's at least a chance . . . Sure mah peekers play all kindsa tricks on me, but at least goin' out thataway I'll know there's still a chance, and thass all we ever want, ain't it? That half-chance, no matter how fuckin' out there it might be. Look at all the folk that flock to the freezin' chambers. Allovum tryin' to escape one death sentence or other. Well, I've paid mah dime an' I've entered they lottery. The lottery of _I don't really wanna die. Not yet._ All that remains is this waitin'.

An' I hope that the fellahs from the Time's Not Up Corporation get here first. Cus thataway at least a bit of the old hope stuff remains. The Milky Bar Kid has shown me the way an' he's shown me good. So I slouch into my barstool, back to the swing-doors and I wait, like they always says you should for a good Guinness. In fact, it's all I can do now is wait. Wait for that tap on the shoulder;

whether it'll be Elvis's security mob or the other lot I s'ppose don't really matter. I won't be round these parts much any more. I juss hope that whoever's in charge of security detail at Time's Not Up Corporation has they head screwed on better 'n me.

Trick Machine

by Richard Evans

karakuri: (n, Japanese) a mechanical device to trick or tease.

Kenji stands outside the bar, takes a moment to preen spiky hair. Deep breath and a last glance at her picture on his Samsung. Dark ringlets cascade around her face. Expressive eyes and a demure smile. He is tense as he pushes open the door. Warm night air surrenders to air-conditioned cool and straight away he spots her sitting at the bar: black skirt: kitten heels, white blouse unbuttoned over low-cut vest. Casual elegance beneath subdued lighting.

"Haruko Mishima

Her alabaster face beams. "Kenji?"

They exchange bows and words tumble out. "Sorry I'm late—I don't know Shinsaibashi too well . . . it's great to meet you at last."

She smiles, glances downwards.

"Like a drink?"

"Neon vodka."

"A girl after my own heart." He catches the barman's eye and swipes his phone over the credit tendril sprouting from the wooden countertop. "Two neon vodkas. With ice and a twist." The barman, lean-faced, nods as he completes the order.

"Let's get a booth."

He picks a path through tables and people to an empty pod at the back of the bar. They sit.

"Smoke?" She extracts a pack of cigarettes from her Murakami hand-bag.

"No thanks."

She lights up and he feels her brown eyes studying him.

"This a regular haunt?"

She shrugs her small shoulders. "No, but friends come here. They tell me good things."

Kenji frowns. "Didn't I read about this place somewhere?"

"It gets a decent crowd—a few *gaijin*, the occasional celebrity."

"Yeah, that's right—this is the bar where they have those *karakuri* girls."

She raises her glass, blue liquid shimmers in the soft light. "Adds a new dimension to people watching, doesn't it?"

"Sure does." He shifts in his seat. "So—it's great to finally meet you. Wasn't sure this was ever gonna happen."

Another sweet smile.

"I've always enjoyed our talks on the eScape."

The bar is noisy, but silence lingers between them. Kenji shifts in his chair, smiles and sighs. The gap persists and eye contact breaks off.

"See that girl?" Haruko uses her cigarette to point.

"Which one?" A discreet scan.

"The one in the strapless top. Big hair." She covers her mouth and whispers. "Big tits." White teeth flash a grin. "With the skinny guy."

"Oh *her* . . . what about her?"

She smirks. "She's one."

"No way."

"Way."

"Get out."

"Wanna bet?"

"Sure." *This is better.*

She opens her bag again and slides a one thousand yen note onto the table between them.

"High roller, huh?" He pairs it with one of his own. "So how do we find out?"

She crushes her cigarette into an onyx ashtray. "Just wait . . . watch what happens . . . Skinny Guy's going to the cigarette machine."

The bartender approaches Big Hair, waving the credit tendril in front of her face. Her eyes sparkle like distant supernovas.

Kenji is aghast.

Haruko grabs the two notes off the table, smiling. "She's got custom-ised Miyagi optics. They're made in Kobe by a couple guys straight out of college."

"Damn, you're good." He pulls a face, faking distress. "There a chance I can get even?"

"Maybe." She raises an exquisite eyebrow. "Let's make it a little more interesting." She places a twenty thousand yen note between them.

He shrugs, reaches into his wallet and matches the bet. He looks towards the crowded bar and gestures. "Take your pick, Haruko-chan."

She leans forward, and Kiyoshi lets his gaze rest on her for just a second. *Much, much better.*

Her right index finger wavers as she makes her choice. "Trouble is, they're so realistic."

"Take your time. I've got all evening to win my money back."

"Eeny, meeny, miny, mo . . . " A slow scan, then. "Black mini-skirt, all legs. Tattoo on her left shoulder."

He follows her gaze. "Talking to the *gaijin* at the bar? No. Way."

"Wait and see."

Each smiles at the other. Neon liquid glistens on Haruko's lips as she takes another sip. "So, Kenji, tell me—you ever been with one of them?"

"Nu-uh." Another headshake. "They look cool but... . . . " he pushes his black hair out of his face and grins, " . . . I prefer real women."

"We can be very difficult."

"Difficult, but worthwhile." A grin then he pauses, thinking.

"I just wouldn't feel comfortable with them—I mean, what's with that eye thing?"

"It's just what happens when they're transferring data—downloading credit or something. I think it looks cool."

"You seem to know a lot about them."

"I'm thirty-four and single." A shrug. "Pays to understand the competition."

He laughs, the neon vodka working his system now. "You know I was so nervous about meeting up. Didn't know how it would be—face-to-face."

"We had to come out of the eScape some time. Curiosity is a great antidote for shyness." She stretches out cat-like, blouse open at the cuffs and neck, giving glimpses of pale skin. The beautiful topography is spoilt by fresh scars along her left forearm. Brown eyes catch him in the act of looking.

"You don't miss much, do you?"

"What's the story? There?" A pause. *Shouldn't have said that.*

Haruko sinks back, hiding in shadows. A long sigh. Silence again, pregnant this time. She lights another cigarette, inhales. Time and smoke spiral. "It was the only way to tell."

"To tell what?"

"They say these *karakuri* girls don't understand what they are." She blows smoke from a corner of her mouth. "It used to be enough to programme them, but not anymore. They feel now. They *want* to be wanted. Desire makes them more committed."

"Committed to what?"

She shrugs, taps ash from the tip of her cigarette.

"So what's that got to do with you?"

"Struck me that if they don't know what they are, then maybe . . . I don't know what I am."

"That's pretty heavy, Haruko."

She holds her arms close to her body and strokes the scars with the tips of her fingers. Cigarette smoke swirls, making her seem like a mirage.

"Only humans bleed."

Elsbeth Schultz

by Rachel Kendall

The girl standing on the platform is weary, but nervous. It is in her pretty, dark eyes. It is in the way her long fingers tug at the braid that falls over one shoulder. She is dressed in a shabby dull grey and obviously feels a little intimidated by the hustle and bustle around her. There are people hurrying past to board the train and she is motionless for a moment, undecided, perhaps, of which direction to take. Finally, with one small suitcase in each hand, she follows the crowd towards the town square.

The marketeers are shouting. The girl walks past stout-looking men selling fruit and veg, old crooked women selling fabrics, a man wavering on a unicycle, a group of young men who seem to stop talking and watch her in silence. When she narrowly avoids stepping in a nest of horse manure on the cobbles, they don't laugh. They just stare. She must look so out of place, so obviously a country girl. She holds her head up and walks past them. When the hot spicy aroma of bratwurst hits her, she remembers that she hasn't eaten since breakfast and stops to buy a small loaf of vollkornbrot at the nearest bread stall. She counts out her money as though it's all she has. When she asks the baker if there might be somewhere to stay nearby, he eyes her suspiciously for a moment, lets his gaze journey the length of her, and then points to a hotel behind him. There is a wooden board clinging to the outside of the hotel by the thinnest filigreed strand.

Die Schwarze Dahlie

She thanks him, despite his rudeness, and takes the crooked path towards the hotel.

On the way she passes a stall of trinkets, framed portraits, masks. White like ivory they are, half-closed eyes sunken into the face, mouths slightly open. All are different, perfectly smooth, glowing like angels. The portraits come in different sizes, showing various people framed in black. Some are children, all share the same angelic serenity.

The girl says these are beautiful. Who are these people?

They are the dead.

This one died in the river. This one was found in a ravine. This Bavarian beauty fell from a window. But they're all anonymous. The woman tries to offer a locket, pushes it into the girl's hand. She doesn't want money. It seems important to her. But the girl is disturbed by the idea and walks quickly away leaving the locket behind.

The Black Dahlia Hotel is a tall building, black on the outside so it looks charred. The door and small window frames are painted white. The windows barred. The girl goes to knock but the door opens and a woman steps out with a small dog on a lead. She looks at her askance, heavy-lidded eyes dark, her step swaggering as though she's just stepped out of an opium den. She takes off, barely looking at the girl, being led, it appears, by the dog.

Inside it is warm and silent, except for the ticking of a grandfather clock beside a small curved desk. A large woman sits behind it and squints at a newspaper. She doesn't notice the girl, who looks around at the staircase ahead and the door to the left, which stands open. There is a subtle scent of incense, something deeply exotic. She puts her bag down on the counter and the woman looks up.

Mein Gott!

She shrieks, gasps, her hand goes to her swollen bosom which is heaving now like an ocean with every hard-pressed breath. The girl gasps and steps back. Her bag drops to the floor, the newspaper falls, and a man comes in through the open door. He stops in his tracks when he sees her, for just a moment, a hair's breadth of a second, and then he is running over to the land-lady.

Are you alright Frau Kellerman?

She is leaning on the counter, her eyes open wide in fear. The man, who is young and well-dressed, takes her by the arm. Frau Kellerman's gaze does not leave the girl's face as the man escorts her through the open door and for a moment both are out of sight. The girl looks around at the pictures on the walls, theatre posters and photographs. The man returns, picks her bag up off the floor and hands it to Louise with a big smile. Are you okay? Oh yes, is she—? Oh yes, he says, with a wave of his hand to trivialise the matter.

> **_Since her husband passed away, you know,_**
> **_she's become a little nervy._**
> **_So, you would like a room?_**
> **_For how long?_**

The girl has no idea. She shakes her head and for a moment looks quite lost.

> **_I'm looking for work and a place to live._**
> **_So I only need a room until then._**

He slides a large book over to her and with a flowing hand she signs her name—Louise Fischer. He unhooks a key from the wall behind him and places it into her open hand. The fob that sits heavy in her palm bears the number 32.

> **_My name is Alaric. If you have any_**
> **_problems you can come to me._**

He is still watching as she disappears from view at the top of the staircase.

Room 32 is quite sparse, the window small. A narrow bed with a metal frame and thin mattress covered by a single thin sheet. A small wardrobe with no hangers inside. A cabinet beside the bed with a small lamp, minus a bulb. The pages in the bible beside it are grey and rumpled like dirty sheets. It is cold. She sets down her cases and then kicks off her shoes. The motion sends a couple of cockroaches running. She shudders, sits on the bed. Stands up again quickly and throws back the covers. No bugs. She climbs in without removing her clothes. She doesn't care that her dress will get crumpled or that she ought to be washing her stockings so they are clean for tomorrow. She is suddenly so tired from the journey. She wraps her arms tight around her body, pulls the bed cover up to her chin and closes her eyes to sleep.

She dreams of her parents. Of their farm. She sees her mother plucking chickens and remembers their stall at the market, how she always liked the smell of the cattle, the way the animals pushed at each other clumsily, the comforting scent of dung and mud and the shouts of the gruff farmers who always smiled at her. She remembers their faces in the car and the car going out of control and the tyres screeching or the brakes squealing and her father, maggoty and black knocking on the car window with knuckles that leave a smear of glaucous dust behind on the glass.

She wakes with a start. The dream fades to black but the knocking continues. It is dark in the room, but for a faint glow through the window from the street lamp burning below. The light sends shadows of the window bars stretching along the thinly carpeted floor.

She climbs out of bed. She shivers. Her shadow stretches across the wall. She is pacing. The noise continues, its intensity growing and coming, she thinks, from behind the bed. She sits and listens, her face anguished in the light. With the knocking another sound begins, a murmuring of low voices. So, the noise comes from the bedroom next door. There follows silence, and then, an almighty grunt, and a vagitus, a spasmodic cry through clenched teeth. Louise stands and goes over to the window, trying to forget the sound as it whittles down to laughter.

She looks out between the bars. She can feel the cool draught of air sliding along the window sill, where the glass has become thicker at the base, distorting the view slightly. Below, the marketeers are packing up. She can hear their bellows and grunts. But her gaze is caught by the church bell tower opposite. It rises high above the sleuth of rooftops and chimneys in a grey sky almost tinged with jaundice. Half way up a gargoyle sits with wings folded neatly onto its back and a snake, writhing and black, spews from its gaping mouth. Louise shudders and strides over to the bedroom door. She throws it open. Across from her, a small man is looking out through the slit of his own open door. His brow is deeply furrowed and his mouth set into a thin, hard line as his hand moves furiously inside his workman's trousers. He turns to her as she gasps in disgust and quickly slams the door closed, a look of revulsion on his face. Louise feels as though she's been caught peeping. This place, this hotel with its verminous clientèle and its insects and its cold, dirty rooms, is trying to leave its stain on her, she thinks. She is more alone than ever.

With a heave, she pushes her suitcases under the bed accompanied by the further scurrying of brown legs. Then she locks the door behind her and descends the stairs. At the bottom she can hear Alaric and Frau Kellerman talking quietly through the open door. She finds them both sitting at a table drinking whiskey. Alaric stands up when he sees her. Frau Kellerman gives a little groan and her hands flutter as if she's trying to dismiss something. Alaric draws out a chair and motions to Louise to sit. As she does he grabs a glass and pours from a pitcher of water. It's as though he's the one running the place.

Louise looks to the landlady.

Are you okay Frau Kellerman?

The Frau snubs her. Looks at her kind of disdainfully. Wrings her hands. Alaric sighs and hands a copy of the Deutsche Zeitung to Louise. She looks at the date—January 1919.

This is two months old.

Alaric nods and urges her to continue.

**The body of the murdered woman found on
Jan 15th has now been identified as 22 year old
Elsbeth Schultz. The police are currently
questioning witnesses.**

Louise looks up, first to Alaric, then to Frau Kellerman who both look to her for a reaction. Alaric points again to the newspaper, showing her something else. A picture, of the deceased girl. Black hair piled high on her head, a heart-shaped face, a small, pretty mouth and black eyes you might lose yourself in. Louise could almost be her twin.

**Do you see why Frau Kellerman is so upset? You gave her
such a fright. Elsbeth was staying here you see. She left
just two days before she was murdered.**

The three sit in silence for a moment. From above, the sombre figures could almost be taking part in a séance, such is the gravity of the scene, the darkly grey tassels hanging from the table cloth, the glass in dead centre, as though placed there by the powers of something unseen.

Suddenly Alaric kicks back his chair and smiles.

**Enough of these long faces. How about I show
you around town, take you for a drink? The
city is really something at night.**

Louise smiles, grateful for his joviality in the uncomfortable silence of the dead girl's memory.

Their footsteps echo around the town square. Her dark grey heels and the swinging hem of her dress; his black trousers and shining black shoes. They tread slowly down winding back streets, past pedlars and beggars and couples out for a stroll. As they cross the river and crawl further inside the blackened nucleus of the city, Louise starts to really notice how these people stare as they pass. How, if she turns her head to look behind her, they are still staring, jaws slack, eyes wide, like waxwork figures in a horror museum.

They cross the tramlines into the furthest and seediest quarter. Here dogs run loose and men stand on corners with cigarettes dangling from fingers or crooked mouths. These men own these streets but they do so with a fight, for on the other corners stand the women. Their advantage is their flesh, so much of it on show, and for such a small fare. Behind them, the buildings seem to mirror that flesh, with their white façades and curving, lace-trimmed bodies. Here, all the buildings are voluptuous, with doors and windows ever open. In opposition, the gentlemen's side is lined with knife-edged brickwork three stories tall that seem to loom like fairytale monsters on scabrous hind legs.

The night is lit up with the billowing flames of streetlights that cause shadows to linger and dance around corners. Alaric spills a little information on the way, the name of this and the history of that. Chimneys, grey in the distance, hold forth like kings over pawns on a chess board and from one, even at this late hour, smoke pours forth into the clouds.

That's the hospital incinerator.
It burns all through the night.

Louise's head is filled with sinister images of the dead and useless burning to powder. Diseased kidneys peeling at the edges, eyes popping and spluttering, hearts cooking.

This street seems to be closing in on them; a pattern of stone archways above and on and on into the distance seem to narrow and lead the eye to the building at the end. The houses on either side lean in towards the girl and her chaperone and the dark windows in each barely hide their staring and pointing subjects. Louise looks around frightened, looks down, follows her feet as they stride across puddles of water from an overflowing gutter. The water runs towards the building ahead as though it were downhill. But it doesn't seem to be. It feels more like an uphill climb.

Oh please. Let's go inside.

Alaric nods and smiles and, taking her by the arm, escorts her to the drinking establishment. Above the door a sign creaks to and fro in a sudden gust of wind.

Der Gehangene Mann

Inside it is warm and crowded, with suited men, and women in raucous make-up. A band play in the corner, the double bass thumping out a warm rhythm; faces dark in the low light laugh loudly; couples sit close and twine fingers, others dance in the centre of the room, oblivious to the less shy and less drunk who watch enviously. Louise has never seen such frivolity; she is caught up in its momentum, her feet wanting to tap. She can't help but laugh, the gaiety of the place conquering her previous fears. After a bad start to the day she feels she might get to like the big city after all.

It is too crowded to sit down, so they make their way to a dark corner, furthest away from the musicians. In their wake heads turn, eyes like spotlights follow Alaric and Louise. Intent on getting to their destination without spilling a drop or tripping over the leg of a chair, neither of them notice the stares. Smudged lips grimace behind painted fingernails, men scuff their shoes against chair legs, whispers carry from mouth to mouth getting louder and more insistent. The couple are oblivious to it all. Louise sucks up her first taste of alcohol.

Who uses the room opposite mine?

She will be bold now. She will not shy away from provocation, if nessecary.

> *Ah, that is Herr Ledermann. Has*
> *he been making a nuisance of himself?*

Louise nods, tries to look worldly, though the thought of that disgusting man . . . It makes the hairs on the back of her neck stand on end. Alaric places his hand on hers.

> *It's nothing to be alarmed about my dear.*
> *He's completely harmless. Soon you*
> *won't even know he's there.*

Well that's a fine thing to have to put up with, but she nods and non-too discreetly slides her hand away and rests her chin in its palm, elbow leaning on a wooden ledge. So much for provocation, so much for being bold. She really doesn't know what more to say about the matter. So she knocks back her drink in three burning gulps. Before she knows it she has a full glass in front of her once again.

> *Tell me about Elsbeth Schultz. Did you know her?*

Alaric looks away, his eyes seem to grow dim as they focus on nothing, just a memory, perhaps, something he has tried to banish. Above him the lights are low, the noise seems to come from far away. He looks thin, ill and worn.

> *No. I didn't really know her. But she was staying at*
> *the Dahlia while I was, so I passed her on the stairs from*
> *time to time. She was very pleasant. Very beautiful.*

Louise smiles, feeling a little more daring now with the drink warming her insides. She slides out of her coat and lets it drop to the floor.

> *And they haven't caught anyone yet?*

Alaric shakes his head.

> *Some say her pimp was responsible. But she*
> *wasn't a whore. She wanted to be an actress,*
> *said she'd met some movie director who*
> *was going to put her in his next film.*

He has become quite melancholic again. While he stares into the depths of his beer, Louise feels abandoned.

> *When they found her, she was in a*
> *bad way. Her body had been cut in two.*

She puts a hand over her mouth as though in shock, but nods at him to continue.

> *The blood had been drained from her body.*

Behind them couples still dance, still laugh. Everyone seems to be singing, drinking, joyous and unconcerned.

> *She had cuts and burns all over her flesh.*
> *She had been bound and gagged.*

Louise pictures the torn body, splayed out with frayed edges. She can see every laceration, every black burn, wrists and ankles chafed, the flesh parted at the waist. The woman is made up of space, a void at the centre of her in to which one might slide a hand and steal a heart or some other gem.

> *Her mouth had been sliced from each corner*
> *to each ear. So she looked like she was smiling.*

She is too hot. The drink is so bitter. She can feel the bile rising in her throat. Somewhere, a glass shatters and a small crowd cheer. Alaric is lost again, looking into the distance, gazing at something only he can see. Does he see Elsbeth now? Is he haunted by her? Louise feels dizzy. There are lights that zigzag in the periphery, a small pain threatens to burst open behind her eyes. She puts her empty glass down on the table and only then does she notice the crowd, en masse, moving forward towards her. They are stumbling over each other to get to her. They move like somnambulists, arms stretched out in front. They are smiling, laughing, every face a portrait of the dead girl, every mouth stretched wider than is surely possible. She stumbles back, bumps into the door which opens onto the street and a rush of cold, damp air. Outside, the rain is like needles hitting her face.

She runs and runs. She doesn't stop running until she is bent over in pain, her lungs scratching her insides and her breath raspy. She looks back but sees nothing, hears no footsteps. Once she has got her breath back, she wraps her arms about herself and walks, hot from running, her legs hurting, her body shaking. She doesn't know where she's going, has no idea where she is or how to find the hotel. The streets all look the same. The town is a latticework of dark stone curved like the back of a beetle. Every few seconds she glances back over her shoulder, sure she heard the sound of a mob. But no one appears, there is no sound but her own footfalls and the rain which has softened to a temperate drizzle.

Up ahead is the entrance to the tunnel beneath the railway line. She will have to go through it, otherwise there is no choice but to turn back and meet her fate. Her hair is loose and whips about her shoulders, she is wet-through in her thin dress. But the tunnel entrance does not look comforting. It gapes like a maw and from here she can see the lump of a body in the strange light, a tramp no doubt, taking shelter from the rain. She breathes in, folds her arms across her chest and takes small steps towards the mouth.

There are lamps lit at intervals. The sleepy flames cast long shadows over the smooth walls scratched in part with names and initials, dates, posters. And there, glaring at her, in darkest black and shining white, her self, her nemesis. A poster calling for witnesses to a murder to come forward. The murder of Elsbeth Schultz. It is the same photo from the newspaper. There is a noise, the scurrying sound of rats. She backs up against the wall. Beside the poster both faces are identical. They could be twins. They could be one and the same girl. She runs further into the tunnel, and it seems she hears the name—Elsbeth—echoing with every footstep. Els-beth Els-beth Els-beth. Ahead of her is blackness, no sign yet of the other side where there is, at least, open space in which to flee in any direction. Here she is captured. She can run only forwards or back, and she doesn't even know who she is running from now. Is it the crowd from the bar who looked intent on killing her (and for what reason?) or is it the dead girl herself, her ghost angry at this mockery of her image?

And then the sound itself is dislocated from its source and stretches down the tunnel, threatening to tighten its chords around Louise's slender neck. Elsbeth is the name she hears and her throat constricts with fear and the agony of what awaits her. They've found her. *Someone* has found her, and he waits at the furthest end of the tunnel. The shout would have the deep resonance of a man's voice but for the sadness that turns it to a melancholy wail.

Louise looks about her. Looks left, looks right. Looks from one end of the tunnel to the other. She steps backwards and leans against the wall beneath a lamp where a trickle of dirty water imitates the roll of a tear down her pale face. She waits. The voice echoes again through the darkness, louder than before, and Louise jams her fist into her mouth and bites down hard. Her eyes wild and bright, the sleeping lump on the floor turning, muffling, and that's when another movement catches her eye. There, just inside the entrance behind her, is a figure. Not a figure but the shadow of a figure. Larger than the mouth of the tunnel, larger than a life-sized man, grotesquely deformed and arms raised above him, a cape or blanket held high; he stumbles forward on his crippled legs.

She screams.

ELSBETH!

The shout from ahead. The sound of creeping footsteps behind. She feels she has no choice but to keep moving forward, towards the voice, a human sound at least. Anything must be better than the beast that follows not far behind. So she steps slowly, keeping close to the wall, hugging it like a cat.

The tunnel is longer than she expected. It stretches further, is more sinister than a life line in the palm of a dead man. It will end abruptly. It will end in death. Mutilation. Rape. All words spell lustmord on the graffiti covered walls.

But finally, she is aware of a different kind of darkness. A less of a darkness. A pale grey spreading, like water, towards her. She can see the end. Summoning up all her strength, anger and fear she runs. She spreads her legs as wide as she can, stretches her strides to cover miles and miles of hellish terrain, running from the footsteps resounding now behind her until . . . suddenly, as she steps out of the tunnel the beast is upon her. It throws its whole weight against her and knocks her flat. She screams. Its tongue lolls and its eyes are burning. It speaks in code—Elsa Elsa Elsa—with the flat broken vocal sounds of a man.

ELSA! You stupid dog.

And it is being pulled backwards, the cord at its neck tightening. It is held by a man. An elderly, withered man, a grandfather, a family man, who is scolding the excitable black dog.

She struggles to stand, but a hand is there to help her. Dark patches of mud cover her dress, her ankle hurts where she twisted it. But these things are overwhelmed by the relief she feels, and her own foolishness in the face of a stupid fat dog with a lolling tongue. She grabs the hand and looks up. It is attached to an arm, to a body and face that belong to Alaric, whose look of concern provides all the comfort she could possibly ask for. She is lifted as if weightless and once on her feet she throws an arm around his waist and buries her head in his chest. The tears course freely down her already-wet face.

He holds her close in a more avuncular than improper fashion, and throws something warm around her shoulders.

You left your coat behind.

He walks her, unsteady as a newborn animal, in the direction of the hotel, while the old man stares at them, trying hard to place the girl he is so sure he's seen before.

A young man and woman stand just inside the foyer. The man leans against the counter, smoking, and the woman stands in a way young women ought not to stand. She has one hand resting on the curve of a hip and all her weight is on one leg, the other stretched out, showing a grey stocking wrapped around a bony ankle. They are motionless and quiet, as though Louise has caught them in *flagrante delicto*. There is just the pulse of the grandfather clock, the pendulum swinging to and fro. She smiles, pats down her damp hair, smooths her muddied dress, and squeezes past them. When the couple notice Alaric behind her, the woman is suddenly all smiles and coquettish flutterings, while the man nods his head ever so slightly, a gesture of respect and un-spoken familiarity.

Alaric takes Louise by the arm and begins to guide her up the stairs.

You know what you need?
What we both need?
A brandy.

When she turns, she sees the man and woman smiling, watching. Did the woman just wave her hand then, wriggle her fingers towards Louise, a sign? Or was she merely brushing smoke away from her eyes? Those same eyes flutter, the smile broadens, the lips stretch and stretch and stretch until Louise looks away with a gasp and clings closer to Alaric.

Are you cold? We'll sit in my room.
Frau Kellerman will have lit the fire for me.

You can warm yourself before you go to bed.

His room is spacious, untidy, warm. There are clothes strewn about as though thrown off in a hurry. There are newspapers folded and torn and trodden-on all over the floor. Some are ripped almost to shreds, others neatly cut in part. A pair of scissors, some unwashed crockery. He makes no attempt to clean up, just points to a chair, mimes that he is going to get them both a drink, and slides out, leaving the door ajar.

Louise takes the opportunity to look around a little. Even snoop, perhaps. She bends to look at photographs, sniffs the cologne on the dressing table, walks around the large bed. Behind it a white drape hangs from ceiling to floor. It gives the room a slightly feminine touch. As she pulls the fabric gingerly towards her, the pin in the top right-hand corner pops out and one half of the drape falls, its weight releasing the other pin. The piece of fabric lands in a crumple on the floor, leaving the wall visible. Louise steps back, bangs her knee on the edge of the bed and stifles a cry. The wall is covered in newspaper clippings, photographs, scribbles, drawings. It is a black and white montage of Elsbeth Schultz. The beautiful glamorous girl with the cupid's bow lips and dark eyes staring out over and over.

It's not what you think!

Alaric is standing in the doorway, a glass of brandy in one hand. On the floor another glass lies shattered, its contents seeping into the wood. Louise hadn't even heard it smash. She turns to him, revulsion hardening her face into inclines and deep shadows.

I loved her.

Alaric is stricken with grief, or fear. This looks very bad, this secret shrine to a dead girl. It makes him a guilty man. Guilty of so many possible crimes. She walks towards him, emitting a low noise like a growl from her throat. She flings her hands into the air, as though she's had enough of this. And suddenly she is reaching down and grabbing the scissors.

Of course you did.
Everyone loved her.

They rise and fall with mechanic precision, pistons in motion. Moonlight glints off the metal blades; the handle hidden in her delicate fist. It seems the motion will never stop, as though she really is an automaton, hidden in the darkness of the room. Repeat, repeat, repeat, until her hand falls wearily by her side, still clutching the weapon as though it has become a part of her flesh. The blades drip thick, black blood on to the floor.

One drop, one heavy, accumulated blister of blood, trickles slowly to the scissors' tip, collects, fights to remain, and then drops, descends and explodes onto the front page of yesterday's Deutsche Zeitung on the floor. Alaric's right hand covers part of it as he lies now heaped amidst the rest of the dirty laundry. But the blood, it has landed splash right next to the smallest article in the most minuscule print, something probably overlooked:

It has come to the attention of the Police that
the murder victim Elsbeth Schultz has a
sister at large. Anyone able to offer any information
regarding the whereabouts of Louise Schultz
is asked to come forward immediately.

Louise stands at the window looking out. The room is quiet, still and heavy. Outside on the bell tower, the serpent continues to gush forth from the mouth of its winged host, like blood from a wound, and down below, the city sleeps as the night closes its jaws around another fateful day.

Girl Absorbed

by Richard Evans

Noriko sits, a girl absorbed. Beneath the old beams inside the spacious A-framed loft, she watches in silence—a full moon shines silver-grey, its pockmarked craters stark witnesses to aeons of celestial abuse. The transitory vision scatters borrowed radiance onto her face through the wide rectangular skylight. Her brown eyes sparkle and she pushes a door wide open and takes a step onto a wrought-iron balcony. Osaka swelters in mid-summer heat, there is movement on streets, rails and expressways below but all she hears is its low roar; distant traffic, far away lives.

Peripheral movement draws her back into the room. Doors shut and seal against the clammy night. The loft's walls are crowded with framed relics from the 20th Century. Diodes draw attention to the collection's most-prized specimens: a letter signed by Lee Harvey Oswald and a priceless fragment of pale lunar anorthosite mounted in a vacuum-sealed box. Other obscure artefacts from the worlds of sport and entertainment are on display, and the space is infused with pop culture authenticity. In a corner, beneath the intense glow of another angled spotlight, Eddie Kuramoto swivels on a high stool, languid in white jeans and a green bowling shirt. Expensive black creepers complete the look. He has a cool confidence; lean, muscular and with a rakish quiff crowning his narrow face. Sideburns trace an outline down along his distinct jaw. Without a word, he extends his right hand and twitches his fingers twice.

She implicitly understands the gesture. She wears a pale blue replica 1950s dress, with a neatly buttoned bodice and a Mandarin collar. Black bangs caress her forehead while the rest of her hair is pulled back into a neat bun. Retro-styled winged spectacles adorn her clear, pretty face. Long lashes blink over her wide eyes and reverentially, she opens the clear plastic container labelled in simple black text: *Apollo XVII*. Using a pair of stainless steel tweezers, she transfers the item as if it is the most delicate thing on earth, sliding the blue and gold cloth badge onto the glass surface of the Veritron. Gears hiss beneath its flat square base, a lens dilates on a hinged arm and a lid lowers, closing over the artefact. Tubes breathe in dust and particles from its surface as an artificial lung sighs in and out. Eddie flicks a switch and together, they watch a network of laser light firing down upon the insignia, revealing its intricate chemical structure in millisecond bursts.

'Wow. This is nearly one hundred years old.' Noriko reads the text on the bottom of the plastic container. 'It was worn by Eugene Andrew Cernan —the last of the first men on the moon.'

'There is some discolouration.' Eddie's eyes fix upon a dark brown stain on the patch's blue background. He calls up a metre-wide projection of the item on his wall screen. Graphs and schematics blink into life. The patch sits side-by-side with an archived mission photograph that features the emblem on the astronaut's uniform. He peers at the stain.

'Says here they landed in the Taurus-Littrow Valley.' Noriko continues. 'Whereabouts is that?' She looks up out of the skylight.

He ignores her and zooms in on loose strands of fabric. 'Maybe it's blood.'

She looks at him aghast and he smiles wickedly.

'We'll know soon enough,' he shrugs.

The Veritron stops breathing with a long sigh. It has concluded the examination and its small red LED display starts a slow countdown. It will be another hour before it reaches a conclusion. Eddie uses the tweezers to extract the badge from beneath the lid and place it carefully back in its plastic holder.

'I heard that people used to say the first moon missions never happened.' Noriko studies the images on the wallscreen.

'So where did that come from then?' He points to the anorthosite sealed inside the vacuum.

Noriko shifts forward, sliding her neat frame off the stool. 'It's late, I'm going to bed.' She moves close and kisses him lightly on the cheek. She can smell his scent, subtle and organic. Her full lips linger for just a second or two. Their eyes meet and she knows that he knows what it is that she wants.

'Night.' He keeps all of his attention centred upon the artefact. She pulls back and slips away, barefoot.

Noriko slumps onto the plush white fabric of the living room sofa. It is nearly two a.m. and she cannot sleep. She draws absentminded patterns across a control pad set into the arm of the two-seater, inadvertently flicking on the Historyweb. Neat bubbles and threads of twentieth century media float in a rainbow of colours before her eyes—pastels and primaries for drama and light entertainment blips, darker hues for old world events and affairs. With a flourish of crimson fingernails, she pricks each sphere back into non-existence.

Fucking Eddie.

Her smooth forehead and delicately crafted eyebrows furrow into a tight knot.

There is a trill from a shape on the elaborate Navajo rug at her feet. Something nuzzles against her exposed shin.

'Hey Jimbo.' She sighs.

Her anger dissipates quickly and she wraps the name in a warm, spoken caress. A canine face peers up at her.

'You are such a good little doggy, but you really should be asleep.'

She strokes the plastic sensor panel on the creature's pearlescent white back and its face lights up with swirling patterns of joyous green.

'Are you a tired baby?' She checks her watch. 'You know you're not supposed to be awake now—we're supposed to be preserving your battery, aren't we?'

Jimbo pants in synthesised excitement, seeming to plead for more attention.

'Oh well, if we keep it our secret, I guess a little cuddle won't hurt.'

She scoops up the faux-animal and pets it with long strokes along its smooth, crafted form. It settles onto her chest and when she is sure that it is soothed, she quietly presses the sleep button at the back of its neck.

'There you are baby, you can have some more love in the morning.'

The room and the night grow silent around her. In this sea of tranquillity, Noriko can hear a voice. It is deep into one side of a conversation. Eddie is speaking to someone on the phone and his tone rises and falls in a lilting cadence. He is laughing. There is a long pause and she thinks it's over, but then he murmurs something again. Her brow furrows some more and her mood slips down into neglect. In a split second, she sets Jimbo onto the rug and creeps back up to the loft.

She stands at the foot of the stairs, quiet as a mouse. The loft hatch is open and she is impaled on every painful word.

' . . . so when can we get together?'

A pause. She can't believe what she hears.

'Tomorrow? You wanna get some lunch?'

He never meets me in the daytime. Always too fucking busy.

'Yeah, *shimesaba* sounds fine.'

He is quiet for a moment and she knows he is paying attention. Noriko listens, bad thoughts filling in the gaps.

'Maybe. We'll have to see.' His voice is lower now. 'Depends if you're a good girl—or not.' He laughs, dirtily.

She hears the phone being set down and wants to barge up there and shout and throw things at him. Rage bubbles instead into silent tears and she turns away towards her bedroom at the end of the long landing.

Noriko sits at the breakfast bar. Newscasts burble quietly from the counter as bright morning sun floods into the white kitchen. Eddie sits opposite, sipping a cappuccino, completely at ease in carefully torn jeans and a white cotton shirt. She hunches her shoulders up before she makes the first move.

'So—was it genuine?'

He looks up from his coffee, puzzled.

'The patch—was it the real thing?'

He shrugs and drains the cup. 'Yeah. I've got a buyer who's ready to pay big bucks for it. I don't want it.'

She mutes the countertop and takes his cup away.

'I was thinking, Eddie, maybe we could meet up today. We could go for a walk at Tennoji Park.'

'Tennoji? Lunch surrounded by all those mangy cats?' He looks momentarily startled. 'Don't think so, honey. Maybe some other time.' He shakes his head. 'I'm in and out of meetings all day.'

Noriko busies herself at the sink. Suddenly, he is behind her, strong arms around her slim waist.

'Hey—you're not upset, are you?'

Comfort comes in waves of warmth. It seems like weeks since he last touched her.

'Look, I know I've been busy lately, but I'll make it up to you, I promise.'

She leans back onto his chest as he kisses her cheek.

'I wish you could take a day off. I get so lonely here without you.'

'You've got Jimbo to play with.'

She turns to look at him and he holds her tight, his fingers massaging muscles in the small of her back.

'But I want you, Eddie.'

He kisses her lightly on the forehead and then pulls away, quick and abrupt, grabbing his black leather jacket from its hook on the back of the kitchen door.

'Gotta go, sweetheart.'

She imagines cupping his cheek with her palm and remembers the feeling of a day's growth of stubble.

'Don't be late.'

He turns and is gone. Doors slam in quick succession as he leaves the apartment without reply.

Noriko stands alone as the empty kitchen comes to life around her, just as it does each day at eight a.m. Water fills the dishwasher, filters clean the air, hidden pumps provide nutrients and moisture to the yucca and ficus plants that line the window sill.

She dozes on the white sofa, her head on plush cushions, her glasses on the floor. The paperback she was reading before she drifted off has fallen down too, with no bookmark to keep her page. She twitches awake with a gasp. For a few seconds, consciousness comes and goes, and then she is present, here and now and looking to the silver starburst clock on the wall for temporal guidance. Seven twenty-four p.m. Her attention moves to the closed-circuit screen set beside the clock and right on cue, she sees Eddie's restored 1953 Chevrolet Bel Air as it makes its way into the basement garage. Its powder-blue presence is like nectar to her senses.

Until she remembers.

Fucking Eddie—

Where he's been.

I'll fucking kill him.

The front door slams. She sits up, determined to ask the question now. There are footsteps in the hallway—footsteps and voices. The living room door creaks as it opens.

Eddie stands there, divine in his leather jacket and ripped jeans. Noriko melts and then freezes back up in an instance. He is not alone.

'Hey Noriko—you had a good day?'

Noriko cannot take her eyes off the woman at his side. A *gaikokujin*; all bangs and Alice band, slim and blonde in a pink cardigan and mini skirt.

Eddie looks confused and the newcomer is silent.

'This is Debbie,' he says at last.

'Debbie?' Noriko repeats the name as realisation dawns slowly. *How could he bring her here?*

'She, ah, wants to look at the collection—you don't mind, do you?' He is smiling and Debbie is smiling.

'Hi Noriko—it's great to meet you.' Debbie leans her head to one side and fashions a nervous wave with her left hand.

Noriko barges between the two of them and, without a word, she storms upstairs.

Dusk is soft through the skylight, casting shadows in a dim orange glow. Noriko sits on the high stool and the tears well up at last, flowing in silence beneath the indifferent stares of dead baseball and movie stars. Her face is in her hands when she hears him ascending the stairs.

Light from the landing below turns him into a silhouette.

'Hey.'

Eddie keeps a couple of metres between them. She wants him to come closer, but she knows she wants to hit him too.

'Was she the one you were on the phone with last night?' Words come in breaks between her tears. 'Was she the one you had lunch with?'

Eddie doesn't look at her and Noriko summons a glare through her fingers, fierce and accusatory.

'What are you doing to me, Eddie? What are you thinking, bringing *her* into *our* home? Don't I mean anything at all to you?'

'Noriko, I'm sorry, it's not . . . like that.' He moves towards her and finally, he holds her in his arms. 'C'mon, it'll be alright.'

She leans into his chest and weeps. Her hands are wrapped into fists, held tight against her body.

'What's wrong with *me*? Have I ever betrayed you? Have I ever deceived you? Don't I look the way you want me to?'

'You know it's not that.'

'Well, what then? What is it?'

'It's just—it's hard to explain.'

She feels his hand moving on her back, at first through the thin material of her white vest, and then upon the smooth skin exposed between her shoulder blades. It is like the touch of an angel, but she wishes he would stop.

'Eddie—don't. We can't.'

'C'mon, it'll be ok. Don't worry.'

His fingers are on her shoulders and she can feel him pressing, kneading, exploring. Her tears dry up and she wishes she didn't feel this way when he touched her.

'Eddie—please—'

His fingers caress her neck now and she looks up at him, her eyes puffy and her body eager. She lets her hands relax as he unravels her. Lips part in anticipation. She surrenders to the grip around her waist and the fingers around her neck. He is over her, around her, everything to her. Noriko's pulse quickens and a rush of excitement courses through her body as he pushes down hard on her second cervical vertebra. A click and a pop and Eddie disappears, along with the loft and the artefacts and Jimbo and Debbie.

It is midnight before she stirs again. Noriko wakes to find herself standing with her left hand resting on the smooth glass of the Veritron. The high stool at her side is empty and Eddie is nowhere to be seen. The room is dark save for beams of moonlight through the window and a strip of light from the angled lamp on the Veritron.

The lid closes with a hiss, enveloping her hand in its glass sheath. The lens whirs, tubes twitch and the solitary lung starts to breathe, slowly in and out, the machine somehow brought to life. She flicks a switch and the lasers fire in a painless dance that illuminates her skin.

'Well, would you look at that.'

Noriko stares, a girl enraptured. Solid skin becomes translucent under the staccato bursts of light, and smooth flesh gives way to a swirl of fibre optics wrapped tight around polymers and a carbon-fibre skeleton. In just a few seconds, the Veritron completes the analysis, its lid slides back and its breathing stops. It sighs out in a death rattle, as if the gift of life was all too brief. Noriko stands with the moonlight and the machine.

'You OK?'

Eddie is behind her somewhere, his voice a whisper. She hears him take a step forward and wonders how long he has been there. She is lost for a moment and then turns to look at him. Like a ghost in the in the silvery light, an apparition amid the relics. Old faces, old letters, dead rock; all bear witness as Noriko looks down at her left hand, still flat on the surface of the machine. Words come to her after long seconds.

'Are we all just mementoes to you, Eddie?'

Her eyes flick toward him and he stares back at her, tight-lipped and unblinking.

'Guess I should have told you.'

'I don't mean a thing to you, do I?' She turns away, runs out towards the balcony, as tears stream down her face.

Osaka swelters still, but there is a breeze now that feels good on her skin. Momentary relief. City lights shimmer beneath under a brilliant moon.

Noriko climbs over the handrail, balancing. She hears Eddie cry out. She rocks on the precipice as he bursts onto the balcony. His hand reaches for her.

The city beckons and she doesn't look back.

Stain

by Rachel Kendall

"I think it's more of a settle than a settee, don't you?"

She presses her spine against the delicately carved back of the seat and strokes the pale green cushion.

"What's the difference?" asks Stu, walking in from the kitchen with two glasses of wine. He hands one to Vivian. His tie is loose, the top of his blue shirt unbuttoned.

"It sounds better!"

"Are you being pretentious or pedantic, dearest?" he asks.

"Oh you know me, I like to call a spade a spade." She motions for him to join her and he perches himself on the edge.

"It's not exactly comfortable," he says.

Though Stu doesn't share Vivian's joy at the sight of the settle in the junk shop, he has to admit it's a fine piece of craftsmanship. Oak, with a high, carved back winged at either end, a two-person bench and storage space beneath. But although it would have looked better in a big old farmhouse drawn up close to the hearth, it doesn't look all bad in their modern house.

"Shame about the woodworm," he says.

"Oh stop picking. We got it for a bloody good price. And it looks so perfect here. Right here."

Right there, where only ten minutes ago the red-faced, slightly sweaty-smelling delivery men had dumped it. At the time the careless offing of their load annoyed Vivian but as soon as they'd gone she'd seen the beauty in the rakish angle. What first looked all wrong now feels very right. And it's a perfect match with the green sash curtains and the plants in large cream pots beside them. It seems very significant and Vivian feels the buzz of satisfaction.

"Have you been buying lipstick again?"

Vivian's left hand is burn-scar mottled in pink and red.

"Rumbled," she smiles, and rummages about in her bag. She brings out a lipstick and quickly applies the dark red without the need for a mirror. She has those perfect bow lips, so natural, so designed for reddening. Stu loves watching her apply lipstick. It seems she could put it on any which way and it would always look right. Those lips that suck the moisture right out of the air, making his mouth dry. They are the oasis that had almost driven him mad with lust in the beginning. He takes the glass from her hand and places it on the floor beside his own. He takes off his tie, and then with his thumb he smears the lipstick across her face before bringing his lips to hers.

There isn't really enough room on the settle for the two of them to lie, but they manage, like young lovers making the most of an opportunity. They have found their symbiosis. Legs and arms plaited, bodies twisted, one inside the other. White skin on white skin in the grey night, they christened their new piece of furniture just as they had christened every room in the house. Newly-weds, they had moved in just two weeks ago, and it seems a rite of passage to fuck in every room and on as many pieces of the furniture as practicable. The bath, the stairs, the shed, the coffee table. They have the thrill of the new running through their veins, semen, saliva. They are boiling over with the fever and fervour of each other and everything one touches the other must touch also.

Stu switches on the light. They hadn't noticed it going dark. They had drawn down the sun with their love-making and then fallen asleep, as exhausted and full as after a feast. He looks at his watch. It is 3am and Vivian, on top of him, is pressing on his full bladder. Her dark hair covers his chest and he feels trapped by the beauty of her. Not wanting to disturb the perfect image. But they both have work in the morning and right now he desperately needs to urinate.

Vivian is hard to wake, numb with sleep. She slides her legs over the edge of the seat like a somnambulist, and smoothes out the pins and needles in her calves. And that's when Stu notices the cushion. Dark red, a port wine stain on an otherwise spotless flesh.

"Fuck," he says. "One of us must have spilled some wine."

Vivian squints, runs her hand over the dark spot. "It's dry," she says. "It's not wine. Maybe it's lipstick. Dammit. How do we get that out?"

"We'll find out tomorrow. Your mum'll know. Come on, let's go to bed. It's late."

Reluctantly Vivian follows him upstairs to their cream and burgundy Ikea bedroom.

"I'll never sleep," she says, "knowing that horrible stain is there."

"Stuart!"

Stu is dreaming. At that moment his head is inside the pink cave of a lion's mouth, but he has tamed the beast and knows, as well as he knows he will die some day, that today the lion will play fair.

"Stuart!"

He is jolted awake and looks over at the radio. It is half six in the morning. Sunlight floods the room.

"What?"

"Get down here."

His eyes are stinging. His right arm refuses to slip inside his dressing gown sleeve without a fight. He grapples his way downstairs on bare feet.

At the living room doorway he stops. Vivian is standing with her arms crossed, fully dressed and immaculate but looking shattered. Or maybe she just hasn't put her make-up on yet.

"What?"

She points to the settle and looks really quite upset. Stu rarely sees Vivian like this. It isn't an emotion she lets others in on, if she can help it. Obviously today she can't.

"For God's sake will you look?"

Stu looks.

One half of the settle cushion, that rather nice mint green, is covered in the same dark red from last night, but lighter perhaps, brighter. The stain has spread. It has grown roots, its tendrils have unfurled, its fingers have stretched out over the edge and now point down to the floor.

"I don't understand," says Vivian, letting the tears now slide down her cheeks. She is shaking her head. "How could it have just grown like that, in the space of three hours? How?"

Stu takes her in his arms. "Hey," he says. "Come on, don't cry. There's got to be an explanation. Maybe it's some weird chemical reaction or something. We'll sort it out babe. Okay?"

She nods in appeasement and then laughs. How silly she is. How embarrassed to be crying over a piece of furniture. It's probably due to lack of sleep. She throws on her coat, kisses Stu goodbye and leaves. Stu should be leaving about now too and he hasn't even showered yet. That stain though . . . He kneels down and puts his face close to the cushion. He inhales as deeply as he dares through his nose. He wants the vinegary smell of spilled wine. Or something else familiar, identifiable. Nothing. He reaches out his hand and presses his palm down in the centre of the stain. Even as he does this, feels the weight of his hand push into the cushion, his heart sinks because he knows that when he lifts his hand the palm will be painted fresh, wet red.

"This is going to be a pretty bad one," says Owen to Greg. Greg hasn't long been on the clean-up team and today would be his worst job. "Single man. Died in suspicious circumstances. Basically we have to get rid of all the shit and keep anything sellable."

Owen has been a cleaner for twenty five years. He's had many partners in that time. They come and go, some last years, others weeks. They hate the stench, the detritus of the poor, the lonely, the sick. But Owen gets a weird satisfaction out of it that no one else seems to get. Being called out to clean up the remnants of a life; making a filthy shit hole into a house again. Erasing death, memories. Removing fleas and cockroaches, rats, used hypodermics, vomit, urine, faeces, rotting food, hard-core porn, blood splatters. Usually a person has died. They had lived alone with neither family nor friends to sort through their material things or aid them in their last days. Sometimes Owen has to sort through heirlooms, bundles of letters, photographs. He has had to throw away items that once held significance to someone, but which are just more rubbish to his team.

Outside the front of number 14 the two men cover their faces and pull on their gloves. Often Owen doesn't know anything about the occupant whose mess he is cleaning up. And usually he doesn't want to know. Sad stories won't help him get the job done. In this case however, he's been given the barest details. The unidentifiable cause of death, the criminal record and the state of the house have given the police cause for concern. But with such a cockroach infestation, the pile of cat shit just inside the front door, and that foul stench that tells of every kind of horror imaginable, the police can't get on with their investigations. So Owen has been called in to ensure the place is safe and free of at least the worst of the grime.

The first thing that catches his eye when they walk in is the settle. He is trained to see the mountains of filth. What he is *not* expecting to see is this magnificent, immaculate, untouched piece of antique furniture pushed against the yellow-brown wall.

"It stinks of jizz in here," shouts Greg from the bedroom. "It's fucking disgusting."

Owen goes over to the settle and runs his index finger over the carving in the woodwork. He gives the seat a good thump. Good, still springy. He opens the doors that conceal the storage space beneath. Empty. Shame. A little woodworm, some small scratches on the inside of the door. Nothing serious. This is definitely sellable.

"Greg," he yells. "Give us a hand." As he pulls the settle away from the wall he disturbs a mass of brown roaches. He begins to pull it towards the centre of the room.

"Greg?" he yells again. "Fucking half-wit," he mutters to himself as he walks into the bedroom.

Greg is sitting on the edge of the bed, surrounded by empty beer cans. He looks up at Owen and then casts his eyes to the small pair of blood-stained underpants on the floor.

"I'll call the police," says Owen calmly, holding down the urge to vomit.

The TV is too loud. The sound penetrates the houses on either side. Both neighbours have been round to complain many times but he won't answer the door. Mrs Carroway even collared him on the street once but he shoved her out of the way so hard she twisted her ankle. She hasn't complained again.

He sits very close to the screen which is filled completely with Simon Cowell's face. Ash falls to the carpet but he doesn't seem to notice. Only when he feels the heat of it on his fingers does he remember the cigarette, and then he just uses it to light a fresh one. He rarely inhales the smoke, just lets it pool up and over his hands. This goes on for hours, night after night. By his feet the remains of a take-away chips and curry is being feasted on by flies. They don't seem to bother him. Even when they land on him, naked as he is from the waist up. They land on his flabby white spongy flesh and he doesn't flinch. His blue braces hang loose on his shoulders and over his small pink nipples. Now and then he stands with a grunt and goes to the bathroom to urinate or defecate on top of the matter already in there. The toilet is blocked and the bowl is filling up. On his return to the living room his eyes are always drawn to the settle against the wall. This was his mother's house and her furniture remains long after she's passed away.

He has never used the settle as a seat. It's too uncomfortable. But the storage compartment has come in useful. Although the doors are closed the image of what they hide from view is sealed in his memory. The small hands, the once-dirty fingernails, the scraped kneecaps that will never heal, the double crown that made the hair grow in all different directions, the small genitals tucked away. The gaping throat.

He sits back down and carries on staring at the television.

The screams of the children echo around the playground. Screams of laughter. The sound of skipping ropes hitting the ground, of footballs bouncing and stones being thrown. The colour of pretend play, the colour of innocence. Screaming bright light of children playing against the grey backdrop of the school.

The man in the car is younger now, thinner. He is sweating and his fingers grip the steering wheel tightly. Although the sun streams in he does not wind the window down. Sunglasses hide his eyes. It is impossible to see who or what he is looking at.

The record turns. Leonard Cohen growls through the speakers. Stu and Vivian sit on the settle. Vivian's legs are curled beneath her and she has a book in her hand—the number one best-seller in the Guardian's fiction list. Stu reads *Private Eye*, letting out occasional grunts of laughter.

By the time they walk in through the door tonight it is 9pm. Stu had met Vivian from work and they'd gone for a Chinese buffet. Neither of them has mentioned the stain. Both of them are shattered from the late night and relieved that it's Friday. It means a lie-in and a further joint exploration into the curves and hollows of the flesh. The stain has spread no further and to Stu's relief is once again dry. He hasn't mentioned the wetness to Vivian as he doesn't want to cause undue worry.

"It's so cold in here all of a sudden," she says, drawing her cardigan tightly around her. They put it down to tiredness and cuddle up closer together. She lays her head on his arm and sighs as the record jumps. Beneath them, the stain begins to shrink. It is becoming fluid, a haemorrhaging mass, is retracing itself, re-forming. Sliding in reverse to its origin, pooling at the back of the settle in the space between cushion and wooden back. It begins to take shape.

"I love our home," says Vivian quietly as she snuggles into the crook of his arm. "I love you. I love us."

Stu smiles and kisses the top of her head. "Me too honey," he says.

Beneath them, liquid trickles and a small, perfectly formed blood-wet hand creeps towards them.

Flat Thirteen

by A.J Kirby

There it was again. That sound. Strange; somewhere between a rickety spin cycle on an old washing machine and the kind of clogged-up death-rattle you get when there's something wedged in the suction part of a vacuum cleaner. A mix of frantic banging and metallic resistance; horrible when you got down to brass tacks and actually thought that the thing might be alive. Might be trapped. But I suppose that's why I'd first compared the sound to everyday objects like a Hoover or a washer. Items which could quite conceivably be found in one of the apartments in our block. Items which might, through some power surge that someone like me couldn't understand but which was still *explainable* in the household scheme of things, make such a sound. Some things do go bump in the night and for no other reason than a mechanical twitch, or an electronic burp.

But there was something else about the sound that troubled me. It troubled me on a level that I wasn't really prepared to acknowledge as a part of my make-up; the fight-or-flight level. The level at which your body acts according to primitive, instinctual whim rather than at the behest of the brain. The level which you reach when the hairs on the back of your neck stand to attention to salute the passing of something otherworldly or evil. I suppose you'd call that level your sixth sense. The thing was, the sound seemed to be coming *simultaneously* from the apartments above and below. It seemed to be coming also from the ones next door and across the hall as well.

I'd managed to block out the downright strange goings on in our block for so long now that ignorance had become a second skin. I was a regular storyteller, such were the excuses I made up to explain that sound. You'll recognise some of them; changes of temperature in the pipes cause them to crack and moan; there were people in the block that worked funny hours or liked to keep themselves to themselves or were agoraphobic. Perhaps the whole apartment complex was some kind of institute for these unfortunates, and only you and I ever stepped out into the open. But surely there would have been some signs; deliveries of shopping ordered over the internet or the odd visitor. Surely.

Of course, I kept it *all* from you. Every bit of it. I suppose part of it was the fact that I wanted you to be happy. Those noises would have been a real stumbling-block for your happiness. But, and I suppose that now it'll do no harm to admit it, it was also laziness on my part that stopped me from telling you. I knew that if I told you about the noises or about the funny goings on in the bin store, I'd be sent to investigate. To *do something about them.* Just like I was told to *investigate* the shower head when I noticed that one nozzle was spraying water in the wrong direction, or like when I noticed that the heated towel rail was faulty. The key to my continued easy life was to simply never tell you anything. So when the noises began—always around that same time at night when you were still at work behind the bar at Chico's—I covered them up. I suffered them in silence.

W hat with the recession and everything, we'd been offered this 'never to be repeated' deal to rent out an apartment in one of the new, prestigious apartment blocks off Boar Lane. You'd done all of the donkey work: visiting the estate agents, arranging the viewing, photocopying the glowing references from our current landlord. That sort of thing. The thing you're so much better than me at doing.

Being my usual unenthusiastic self, it was all the effort I could muster to drive us into town and deposit a veritable treasure chest of coins into the parking meter. But I made you understand that these simple tasks *were* an effort for me. A constant barrage of sighing saw to that. And the snapped answers to just about every question. You ably shrugged off my sulk. Your excitement saw to that.

'I've always wanted to live in town. The bright lights; the activity; the *people*,' you gushed as we walked away from the car. You seemed to be wilfully ignoring the fact that we'd had to park in some dingy back alley *and* pay for the privilege. I suppose that you were looking beyond what was immediate and looking at the horizon; the tasteful neon lighting, the sculpted walkways and gardens. The balconies. The restaurant at the bottom of the block.

'What time's the woman meeting us?' I asked, not really caring about the answer unless it was a time that wouldn't suit me. Say if she kept us waiting out in the blistering November cold for more than five minutes . . . Then I'd be able to let rip with the sum total of all of my frustrations.

'In about twenty minutes,' you answered. 'I thought we'd have a look around the rest of the area while we wait. Get accustomed to our surroundings.'

You beamed encouragingly.

I sighed, but stayed my tongue. Not yet.

I trudged after you as you walked through the large archway which marked the entrance to the new development. I couldn't remember the last time you'd walked ahead of me. Usually, you walked so slowly, wanting to look at everything, wanting to touch, smell, and taste. I was usually the one that powered ahead with that long impatient stride of mine. But you had a spring in your step that night. Even with your heels on.

You'd dressed for the occasion, which despite my condescending attitude, I couldn't help but find sweet. Even though they could barely give these apartments away, you feared that we might be black-balled because of our dress sense or because we weren't cool enough to live in town with all of the young urban professionals: the test-tube baby lawyers and the *Star Wars* accountants. I skipped a little in order to keep pace with you as we stepped along the large central courtyard in the between the two apartment blocks.

The whole courtyard was lit up like a Christmas tree. Little acorn lights spilled over the branches of every newly-planted sapling, little fake-star lights pock-marked criss-cross wires which we weren't supposed to be able to see. More light washed out from the frontage of a couple of shops and of course the restaurant at the bottom of the block: Chico's.

I'd been to Chico's once before, although not with you—with work. Celebrating the sign-off of a new piece of software which I'd tailored especially for a big client. He took us there by way of a thank you and to make sure that in the event of anything going wrong, I'd be on hand to set it right within a set timeframe. He seemed to keep repeating this point throughout our uncomfortable evening. And when I say uncomfortable, I don't necessarily mean because of the company, although that didn't help. I mean because the whole place seemed to carry this tremendously negative attitude. It was tangible, crackling over the loud-speakers in time with the faux Italian music. In the over-elaborate mirage chandeliers on the ceiling. The whole place just seemed too *temporary* for my liking. I kept thinking that if I reached out and touched the exposed brickwork of the walls, I'd find them to be made out of cardboard. And behind the set would be the developers, sniggering into their hands about the fact that they'd made fools of so many of the city's supposed shining stars. I knew what would happen if I looked too closely behind the scenes of the shiny new development. It was all about surface, and a very *thin* surface at that. It wasn't built to stand the test of time, just that instant moment of *now*.

Wearily, I looked at my watch. *Now* was moving very slowly. I'd never been good at waiting or at simply doing nothing. Without my crutch of a cigarette, I had nothing to lean on in those cold moments outside the apartments. I looked at my watch again, hoping that I'd somehow misread it the first time.

'Stop looking at your watch,' you sighed. 'Just look around you. Can't you just imagine us living here?'

In truth, I couldn't. I was telling you about the *temporary* feeling that the whole development seemed to contain. And sure, that was eerie. But when you spoke and it echoed off the concrete of the apartment blocks, that struck me as even weirder. Wasn't this place supposed to be some kind of bustling arena for the young and beautiful of the city? Weren't there supposed to be mime artists lining the walkways, trapeze artists swinging through the sapling trees, and groups of people on benches discussing existentialism?

Wasn't there supposed to be the constant buzz of things going on, things being created—life?

The courtyard was dead. Dead echoes attached themselves to our voices.

'You know, I just don't think that living in city centres is the same here as it is in the US and places like that,' I said. 'I mean, in the US you get families in the apartment blocks. Here, it's like a stop-off point between university and real life. I don't think you find many people over forty living in the city centre. All a bit transient . . . '

You raised your eyes to the fake stars.

'Look. If you've got a problem with us moving into the city centre, tell me now, before it's too late. Before we move in and you then use it as a grudge against me.'

I coughed with embarrassment. You'd hit the nail slap-bang on the head as far as my plan was concerned. Not that it was much of a plan.

'Doesn't hurt to look at the apartments,' I conceded. 'See how many rooms it has. That sort of thing . . . '

'You should already know that,' you hissed. 'It was in all of those emails that I forwarded on to you. All the picture attachments . . . '

'Oh yeah,' I said. 'I remember now . . . Erm. Is that the woman we're meeting?'

I pointed off over her shoulder, glad of a chance to change the subject. A woman had stepped through the gateway and into the courtyard. She was dressed in a long grey rain-mac; looked like a man's, but was so tight-fitting. Her high-heels hammered against the paving stones. She walked almost as impatiently as I did.

'Looks like her,' you agreed. 'Not like there's anyone else here so we could get confused.'

So you had noticed how unnaturally quiet it was. How ghost-town deserted. If we stayed here long enough, we'd probably see the tumbleweed come spiriting past.

The woman approached us and immediately extended her hand to me, ignoring you. She'd already got us worked out all wrong. She thought I was the decision-maker.

'Rachel Goodhind,' she said, jutting out her jaw-line aggressively as I grasped her leather-gloved hand. Whenever anyone wore leather gloves I always thought they had something to hide. A fake hand perhaps, like Luke Skywalker in *Star Wars*.

'Mallory,' I said, trying not to look at the bottom of the woman's face. 'Dave Mallory.'

The woman sensed my unease. She knew that close-up, people didn't really want to contemplate those grotesque features. The underbite, which was no so much pronounced as shouted. And it wasn't just shouted, it was *spelled out* in the same menacing tones that a determined English tourist would use to try to explain a particularly difficult concept to a foreigner.

'You're here for Flat Thirteen?' she asked, rifling through some paperwork on her clipboard. Her voice was posh, helped no doubt by the mangled underside of her face. Rich people often spoke in this drunk-sounding blur, I found.

'We are,' you agreed, immediately asserting your authority. I happily stepped back and allowed you to speak to the woman. My eyes flickered over her wire-brush hair. Her earrings like shields. Absently, I wondered what the hell a woman from such a presumably privileged background was doing working as a common-or-garden estate agent. I wondered if she was happy with her life. Surely women such as her were only happy living with their rich landowner husbands who beat them within an inch of their lives while they looked after his big-cocked dogs.

Suddenly, I realised that both of you were looking at me, heads cocked to the side like suspicious pigeons.

'Ready Dave?' you asked, with that warning look in your eyes that you always got when you thought I was going to say or do the wrong thing.

'Sure am,' I lied.

The woman fell into step with me as we crossed the courtyard to the block which was pretentiously dubbed 'One'. The block which we'd be calling home. As she talked at me about how 'desirable' it was to live in that part of the city and how much money had been pumped into the development, I gazed bleakly at my shoes and reassessed my opinion of her. I decided that she was a determined soul. And she *was* the sort of young woman that could be described as a 'soul', too. She wouldn't have seemed out of place in an Austen novel, or perhaps in *Black Beauty*. I longed to ask her if she rode horses and whether this was the reason her black-grey hair ruffed up at the bottom as though it had been confined within a helmet for far too long.

We stepped through a heavy, access-controlled front door and entered 'One'. I could smell the fresh paint on the walls; could feel the re-cycled heat of the aircon; could hear the squeak of my shoes on the virgin wood flooring.

You gasped.

'I know,' mangled Rachel. 'Looks just like a hotel lobby or something, doesn't it?'

And it did. There was a grand, red-carpeted central staircase which peeled off into two separate stairs leading up to the apartments. A marble-topped reception desk, behind which were lots of numbered mailboxes. By the door, the floor was polished wood, but near to the great glass elevators, it was beautiful mosaic. It looked like an elegant New York hotel from the last century; any minute Holly Golightly would dance down the stairs. Darling.

'Oh this is wonderful,' you whispered to me.

Rachel looked on indulgently. I hated her for it. She thought us fools that would be seduced by the mere sight of such glamour. I decided to break the spell.

'How many of these apartments are actually taken?' I asked.

Rachel hesitated. Only momentarily, but the pause was there all right. I'd asked the difficult question.

'I'll level with you,' she said, chin anything but level; collapsing all over the place. 'Off the record, there are about three hundred empty apart-ments in this development alone. Throughout the city, and with all of the building work that's still going on, you could add a couple of noughts to that figure. Supply far outweighs demand, and that's why you're in such a good po-sition. That's why the two of you can call a palace like this home for probably half the price that was originally intended.'

I'd heard similar figures. When the initial rush to live in city centres started, I think everyone just got carried away. Everyone saw pound signs in front of their eyes and didn't stop to consider the possibilities. They built and built and built before even stopping to consider where they'd find the people to fill all of those 'desirable living spaces'.

'Let's go look at the apartment, shall we?' you asked.

I didn't move.

'Seeing as though you've already told us that there are plenty of apartments free, can't you show us a different one. Not that I'm superstitious, but Flat Thirteen? Seems kinda like not the ideal choice . . . '

Rachel Goodhind smiled. It was a terrifying sight. Right then I would have *bought* Flat Thirteen, crippling mortgage or not, just so I wouldn't have to see her do it again. It was as though her whole face collapsed in on itself. Or like she was one of those old men in backward Lancashire towns that compete in gurning competitions.

'Flat Thirteen,' she whispered, as though letting us in on a tasty little secret, 'was the one that the architect designed for himself. He meant it to be his home. So it's not like any of the others. It's special.'

'So, why's he not living there then?'

Rachel paused again. This time it took longer for her to unwrap her face and speak again. It was as though a shadow passed over her. As though there was something that she didn't want to tell us.

'Mr. Rooney grew a little, uh, *disappointed* when the block wasn't filled up as quickly as he'd hoped. He'd envisioned a living space like the New York apartments by Central Park. He'd wanted families in here. Children. The peal of laughter. He didn't like it cold and empty. He decided to, uh, go away.'

'Go away?' you asked.

'Yes . . . Anyway I mentioned that he wanted families to live here. So he provided plenty of on-site things to do. The pool: this is one of the only blocks in the city which has its own pool. And the gymnasium and weights rooms.'

You began to be washed away by the woman's sales spiel again. You ignored the strangeness of the story that Rachel had started to tell us about the architect. You were entranced by the *idea* of living at 'One', and you wouldn't let anything get in the way of that. Before I could say anything else that might ruin the moment, you started to drag me across that squeaky wooden floor towards the elevators.

The elevators smelled new, of course. Probably they'd only been used two or three times before, as tests. There were nice, homely touches in there too, which you couldn't resist pointing out to me as we ascended. Flowers, obviously fake, on a mahogany table in the corner. Tinny muzak playing over the tiny speakers which were installed in the corners of the roof. Rachel Goodhind pressed her nose against the glass and looked out over the black liquid of the river flowing below us. From the almost haunted look that crossed her face, I could have sworn that she was about to smash through the glass and throw herself in.

Soon one of the numbers became illuminated. Silently, the elevator swooshed to a halt. We'd reached the third floor. Not quite penthouse, I thought, but didn't say. We stepped out of the doors, me going last like a proper gentleman. As I followed you out, I felt my feet slipping into the arterial red carpet of the corridor. Another nice touch, I thought, before I realised that what the red carpets and the elevator doors actually reminded me of was one of the most striking scenes in Kubrick's *The Shining*.

'All work and no play makes Jack a dull boy,' I whispered to myself as I trotted behind as meekly as the little lost puppy. Luckily, you were too excited to pay me any attention. At the end of the corridor, Flat Thirteen's door could clearly be seen. And the doorway was magnificent, like one you'd find at the front of a stately home, complete with this big brass horse-head knocker.

Rachel fished a gaoler's set of keys from her handbag and tried a couple in the lock before we finally heard the gratifying click which meant that we were in. You sprinted through the door to get the first look at the place. I meandered in last.

Breathless, you stood in the centre of the room and took in the vast panoramic window which made up an entire wall of the flat. You reached behind you for my hand, without even knowing for sure I was there as you looked up, saw the mezzanine floor, the wide-screen TV and theatre-style seating area. You could barely contain your joy at the sight of three or four doorways leading off the main room.

'Just wait until she sees the bathroom,' whispered Rachel, menacingly.

The bathroom was a palace, complete with a jacuzzi, individual sinks for man and wife, a walk-in shower which could have quite easily accommodated a whole rugby team with room to spare, the dreaded heated towel rail affixed to the wall.

'We have to have this place,' you whispered.

Tellingly, Rachel winked at me from the doorway, where she was nonchalantly leaning, doing something strange to her mouth. Suckling, almost. She could smell the blood of her commission off us. She could smell another barnful of hay for her horses, or whatever it was she spent her money on.

'Let's just take a look at the bedrooms,' I whispered back, hoping against hope that there would be something awfully wrong with them. Like we'd walk in and there'd be a huge king rat on the bed, cleaning guts and gristle from his claws. Or a cockroach crawling along the bed-head. Or a dead body in one of the wardrobes. Perhaps the body of the elusive Mr. Rooney, the architect.

Rachel walked with confidence now, hips swaying, her grey mac slung over her shoulder and held by a single, red-clawed finger. She had no doubts. As she threw open the door to the master bedroom, I heard that suckling kinda sound coming from her Sarlacc pit mouth once again. The room was disappointingly wonderful. Untouchably pristine. Masterfully designed. It was like something out of an MTV *Cribs* show.

Without even looking at you, I said to Rachel: 'Where do we sign?'

I always spent more time in the apartment than you did. I basically signed over my soul to the Jackson and Jackson Estate Agency that day; I very rarely seemed to have a life outside Flat Thirteen after a while. Flat Thirteen *owned* me, I suppose, in a way that even CS Software never did. And even if I did leave the flat, there was no need for me to ever leave 'One'. The swimming pool and the weights room were too handy. The concierge was too good to me. It was all too comfortable.

I got more work done—and more *productive* work—done there than I'd ever done in the office or in our old suburban rented house. In the flat, there was no office small-talk to distract me; no disturbances from Old Mrs. Stubbins from next door telling me that her little cat had gone missing again.

I was able to write glorious software. I know you always found it hard to understand, but software *can* be glorious when it functions. Some programmes I delivered were so perfect that I could hardly bear to part with them. They were programmes about which people would say: 'I honestly don't know how we coped before.' They were beautiful. Life was beautiful. Or easy, at any rate.

When the noises started, I paid them no mind. They barely even registered on my radar. If they weren't coming from anywhere in our flat then they didn't matter anyway, did they?

But soon, of course, the noises got louder. Soon, I couldn't ignore them. At first, I told myself it was the sound of other residents, or building work. But there was never any sign of anyone else in the blocks, especially not builders or the mess that they frequently leave behind. There never seemed to be anything but mass mail leaflets in any of the other mail-boxes either. And when I'd tried buzzing on 'One's' other doors, there'd been no answer.

Now this, to an early thirties bloke that's been used to having to keep the noise down after eight o'clock at night in case he woke Mrs. Stubbins was like freedom itself. An adventure. Being so *alone* in the block of flats; being able to do exactly as we wanted was delicious. Need some Metallica at full blast (as it should always be played in my opinion) but at 5am when you've just finished writing the final part of the software programme? No problem. Certainly no problem from the neighbours. Need some bed-head-smashing-a-gainst-the-wall sex at 8am? Again, no problem. And how would sir like to watch a horror film later, so loud that the screams reverberate through the whole block? Good; that's fine sir. And don't worry about your bill. You can settle that *much* later.

As I said, life was easy. But you didn't seem to want easy. You wanted something else. One night, when I'd come down to Chico's at the end of your late shift for a drink I sensed there was something wrong. You'd become so vague about everything. You'd even forgotten what lager I drank, which was very unlike you, seeing as though you always complained about the amount of bottles I left around the flat. I asked the dreaded question, unable to stop myself, like a lemming whose mates have just flocked over the edge of a cliff.

'Are you all right? Is something wrong?'

You sighed, wiped your hands down on the end of your black corduroy apron and gave the most pathetic attempt at a smile that I'd ever seen.

'Fine,' you answered, ringing up something on the till but then forgetting why you'd even approached the till in the first place. I saw your eye begin to quiver.

'Come on; you can tell me,' I prompted.

'Nothing's wrong,' you said.

And that, I thought, was the end of it. More fool me. Later on, when I'd taken a seat at the back of the restaurant and you were up cleaning the tables down, you let me have it with both barrels.

'You're right,' you said. 'There is something wrong. *This.*'

You gestured around you. I thought you meant the mirage chandeliers, the fake brickwork, the terrible muzak which I was actually starting to get used to. A little.

'You can always get another job,' I soothed.

You slammed your tea-towel down onto the table in front of me, almost knocking over my lager.

'I don't want another job. I just want a different life. I want something other than this. The same days over and over again. The never going out any more . . . '

'We do go out,' I interrupted, foolishly. 'What are we doing now?'

'I don't mean staying for a drink after work. I mean going out. Seeing people. Seeing our old friends. Having a laugh. Like we used to do. We never see people.'

You pointed out of the window, to the empty courtyard. You were right, I suppose. When it got dark around here, you were basically looking at a bonafide ghost apartment block, if not a bonafide ghost town.

'Well, how about we go out for your birthday next week?' I asked. 'How about we call up some of those *friends* that can't even be bothered to come down here and see us? See if they'll come out if we go to a nice bar in the city centre.'

You smiled gingerly. And right then, I knew it was fixed. I knew that we'd have to go. How could I have been so stupid as to fall for your act? Somewhere in the bowels of 'One', or in the rafters or on the stairs, something moved. It rattled with anger at our decision. Inside Chico's, I could hear the din. I stole a surreptitious glance at you to check whether you had too, but it appeared that you hadn't. You were already too preoccupied with the organisation of this birthday night out.

L oath as I am to admit it, I'd been dreading the birthday night out for a week. And as seems to be the case with everything that you dread, it looms onto the horizon quickly; it's upon you before you even 'have the chance to prepare yourself. Time conspired against me, I suppose. It made wicked little plans and hatched sneaky little plots so that the cogs and wheels of my watch moved with unnatural speed. Before I knew it, I was welcoming your friends Bev and Martin into our safe haven and watching them lay their sticky fingerprints over everything that was precious. It was all I could do to _not_ follow them round with a window cleaner when they persisted in pressing their noses against the panoramic glass and cooing over the view.

Of course, we weren't talking. Not to each other anyway. The argument was on account of the fact that I'd persisted in calling Bev and Martin 'your friends' and not 'our friends'. Stupid. But you talked to them. You told them all about what a good deal we'd got on the flat and how we'd got this picture perfect life nowadays.

'Everything's here on our doorstep,' you said. 'You should have a think about moving here too. There's loads of flats still going spare and I'm sure that if we had a word with our estate agent, Rachel, she'd be able to do you a good deal.'

Creaking. Moaning. Choking sounds from the depths of the block. I had to cough loudly and then turn up the music with my remote control just to cover the sounds up.

The awful Martin approached me, obviously sensing my unease. I was absolutely convinced that he was going to start asking me about the sounds, or whether we had a problem with our plumbing, or the neighbours.

'You okay there, Dave?' he asked, pushing his glasses back up his nose as though to take a closer look at my obviously ashen face.

'Just raring to go, that's all,' I said. 'It's been a long time since the pair of us have been out. We've had a lot on . . . '

'Busy with work?' asked Martin, and I immediately allowed myself to switch off. Dave was the kind of person with whom you knew that anything you said would be immediately twisted around onto his favourite subject of work. And Martin was the kind of person that *just knew* that his own job was more important, more time-consuming, and more skilled than anyone else's. I honestly don't know how I got through that next half-hour with him, but I did. And the only reason I know that is because soon we were all bundling into a taxi and all shouting at once the name of the bar that we were going to.

At Smilla's, we met more of your interchangeable friends. I'd started drinking at a rate of knots by then, just to drown out the sounds of creaking and groaning in my head, so I can't really remember. Perhaps it was Kev and Marion and Nev and Marlene. Maybe it was Trev and Nev. I don't know. All I could hear was this *whooshing* sound every time one of them opened their mouths to speak to me, like the sucking of a Hoover, only louder. Then rattling, too, like there was something within Bev or Kev or Trev that was trying to get out, or was being sucked in. Their death's rattle voices told me everything that I needed to know though; I shouldn't have left 'One'. Something indescribably terrible was going to happen because I had.

You took me to one side as I staggered back from the gents.

'That was the ladies you went in,' you hissed, gripping my arm far too tightly than was strictly necessary.

'Was it?' I asked, vaguely, trying to wrack my brains to remember if I'd pissed in a urinal or a sink or a proper toilet. Despite the booze and the sounds in my head though, I could still think of a speedy answer when required, and I slurred that I'd thought the toilets were unisex. You raised your eyes to the ceiling, but in fairness my lie *was* conceivable. Smilla's was the kind of pretentious bar that didn't mark prices or labels on anything, especially the precious drinks and bogs. It was modelled on a snow scene or something; apparently you'd read the book once. Of course, it was a highly popular place in the city centre.

'Just slow it down on the drinking,' you said, chancing a breezy smile in my direction.

That smile nearly blew my head off. Even the smile had a sound of its own. It was the clanking, grating sound of chains being shaken. I had to close my eyes to try to block it out. You must have thought that my head was spinning or something. I felt your arms on me, more gentle this time.

'I'm okay,' I gasped, craning my eyes open. Hearing the noise again.

'I'll go to the bar and get you an orange juice or a glass of water,' you said. 'Something that'll re-hydrate you. Just wait here.'

I did wait there. I waited with my head cracking against the wire-mesh pretend-snow walls of the corridor to the toilet. I discovered that if I banged my head against the wall in time with the groaning sounds, the sounds somehow didn't rip into my ears as much.

Then, just when I thought everything was going to be all right, I opened my eyes, and realised that what had gone before was actually a milder level of hell. I'd now descended to the realm where monsters roamed. A woman was leaning against the corridor opposite. She was wearing a masculine-looking grey coat. Her wiry hair was scraped up into a painfully tight bun and her make-up looked as though it had been rollercoastered onto her face. Only, the make-up couldn't disguise that terrible mouth of hers. The jaws of hell.

'Hello, Mr. Mallory,' said Rachel Goodhind. 'And how is she treating you?'

Like a drowning fish I gasped and gulped but took in no air. My limbs trembled. I felt the urge to revisit the ladies toilet.

'She's . . . she's treating me fine,' I gasped, finally. 'Actually, it's her birthday. We've come here with some of her friends.'

'Not your girlfriend, Mr. Mallory; I mean the flat. Flat Thirteen. How is she treating you? I used to live there myself, you know, not long before you moved in. Not long at all, in fact.'

'You used to live in Flat Thirteen?'

'I did,' said Rachel, proudly. 'And it was all I could do to give her up, but I needed the commission, you see, so I had to let her go.'

All I could do was stare at her. Close-up, she had the kind of pale, papery skin that suggested recent or forthcoming bouts of eczema. The questions bubbled up within me, but I couldn't find the right ones to ask. Rachel Goodhind knew though. She knew.

'You're hearing the noises then? Good. That's a good sign. Don't worry about them. They're good for you actually. Haven't you found that your life is better than it's ever been since you moved in? Your work, too?'

Somehow, I found myself answering: 'I have. But what *are* the noises? Is it something to do with Mr. Rooney? Why can't anyone else hear them?'

'Oh, Flat Thirteen's a fussy little madam. She only really takes kindly to one person at a time. You should be glad she chose you . . . the trouble we had when we were there . . . '

'We?' I panted. I stole a quick look over my shoulder to check whether we'd been spotted by any of your friends or by you. But we were safe in our little purgatory of a corridor and its shiny-tiled floor. Amazingly, nobody had even squeezed past us to visit the toilets, despite Smilla's being more packed than I'd ever seen it.

'Mr. Rooney and I, of course,' grimaced Rachel. She made that clogging, sucking sound with her hell-gate mouth and it was all I could do to cling on to the edges of known reality with my fingernails. 'Goodhind's my maiden name . . . Oh, you really don't know anything, do you Mr. Mallory?'

I shook my head.

'Suppose I'd better tell you the story then. Just so you know what to expect. Poor old Mr. Rooney deserves that much, I suppose . . . '

I longed to ask her why she insisted on referring to the man who had quite clearly been her husband by the formal version of his name. But I figured that particular puzzle was most likely the least of my worries. I figured there were far more pressing questions that needed answers.

'He was an obsessive, you know,' continued Rachel. 'Just like you probably are. Just like I am. When we first saw the site for the development of "One", all it contained was a few old buildings which used to service the waterways—warehouses and the like. Mr. Rooney was particularly taken by one of the buildings though. He kept calling her "the one".'

I nodded, reduced to simple head gestures now.

'Anyway, he decided to gut the building and develop the first of his great apartment blocks _within_ its existing framework. Said he felt drawn to it. . . . Of course, I knew that there were other, more reasonably-priced plots of land, but there was no persuading him otherwise. He designed that place morning, noon and night. Sometimes I'd go into his study and take a quick peek at his drawings. All he kept saying was that he'd suddenly found the glory in his work. At the time, I didn't understand. When the planning permission came in and work started on the building, he worked even harder. Eventually, he decided that he couldn't even be away from the place at night. We sold our country pile and moved into a specially-designed apartment, Flat Thirteen. Like you, I didn't like the fact that he'd chosen a number so weighed down with significance.'

'But what happened to Mr. Rooney?' I cried, finally unable to take the pressure any more. I _had_ to know.

Rachel raised one eyebrow at my rudeness, but continued nonetheless. She continued in a hushed, restrained manner. Amazingly, I could hear her above the self-satisfied hum and buzz of Smilla's.

'Something terrible happened. At almost exactly the same time as he started to hear the noises most loudly, I became pregnant. For years it had been all we'd wanted. Remember what I said about Mr Rooney wanting to hear the sound of children laughing and building the pool and entertainment rooms for them?'

I nodded, solemnly.

'And then the noises became voices. And the voices were jealous. Flat Thirteen was so used to Mr. Rooney whispering to her in the middle of the night about how special she was that she couldn't stand the thought of something else becoming the apple of his eye. Eventually, she told him that she wanted him to push me out of the great glass elevator and into the river. She told him that the body would never be found and that they could live happily ever after together. I don't know what happened—inside his mind, I mean—but one day when we were in the elevator, he grabbed me by the shoulders and screamed in my face that he was going to kill me. But before I even got the chance to get properly scared—part of me still thought he was joking—he jumped through the glass.'

'Into the river?'

'When the police came later,' she said, remaining almost chillingly calm, 'they told me that they were amazed that the building had even been passed fit for habitation. The glass in the elevators, you see. He'd not even got the builders to fit reinforced glass . . . He'd known what was going to happen all along. He was a hero. That's why I always left the flowers in the elevator . . . To remember him. When I had to move out, that's when I put in the fake flowers that I heard you comment on.'

'What happened to the child?' I asked, unable to stop myself.

'Given up for adoption . . . after the other accident.'

'What other accident?' I breathed.

Rachel simply pointed to the underside of her face: the mangled chin, the pronounced underbite and that weird suckling shape that her mouth took when she thought nobody was watching. I closed my eyes, already hearing the pressure of the noises coming back into my head. When I opened them, Rachel Goodhind was gone. You were in her place, that worried look on your face again.

You held out a glass of water to me and ordered me to drink. I think that must have been when I screamed, but I'm not really sure. The sound might have been coming from far away, across the other side of town; from 'the one'.

Back at 'One' all was quiet apart from the soft pitter-patter of rain on concrete. The sky had bruised-over though, and threatened a storm soon. But in the drizzled darkness of the night, in the heavy blackness of time, something moved. Something stepped up to the plate and started practising its swing. Big loping curves were chiselled through the air. All hell was about to break loose.

You couldn't feel it. You didn't sense that slight trembling in the ground. Some people have a sixth sense for these kinda things; like the people that claim they can *smell* thunder, I suppose. Right then, I was one of them. I could see the evil trailing like smoke from the rooftop garden of 'One'. I could taste its seductive spice. We walked in silence, but in my head, I communed with Flat Thirteen. I asked her what it was, exactly, that she wanted me to do.

For the first time, she answered me in a language that I could understand.

'Kill her,' she whispered, her soft tongue somehow tickling my earlobe. 'Push her through the glass. The glass is still weak. Make her like stupid Rooney. Then we can be together. Then you can write your glorious software. Then you won't have to go to places like Smilla's again.'

I put my hands over my ears. I couldn't help it.

I screwed up my eyes.

I stayed my mouth.

See no evil. Hear no evil. Speak no evil.

You must have thought that I'd finally stepped off the end of the pier and entered that vast ocean called madness. You must. Because you started to drag me towards the glow of Chico's Restaurant. I saw little Chico himself step out, dressed in penguin black and white. He looked as though he were a child trying on his father's clothes. But his face looked like that of a gargoyle. I jumped backwards like a startled horse.

'Not in there,' I whispered. 'Up to the flat.'

'Yes. Up to the flat. In the elevator. Push her through the glass,' whispered Flat Thirteen. I felt her teeth start to nibble at my ears. It was impossibly sexual. I felt like I was about to burst out of my trousers at any moment.

Somehow, we managed to get through the door entry system despite the fact that my hand was trembling so much I could hardly hold the key-fob properly. The concierge gave me a withering look from behind the marble desk but I ignored him. It was quite easy to ignore him considering the fact that there was a porno flick *and* a horror film playing simultaneously in my head.

We called the lift. Naturally, it was already waiting for us where we'd left it, like an obedient dog. For once, part of me wanted there to have been other people in 'One'. Other people that might have left the lift on the fourth floor, so I had time to try to get my head straight.

No such luck. The doors *binged* open and we both stepped in, you giving this semi-relieved sigh that told me you believed the worst was over, me giving this strangled moan which should have told you that far, far worse than you could ever have imagined was still to come. Robbie Williams was playing tinnily over the ceiling-mounted speakers. 'She's the One', I believe it was. And never had that revolting song sounded so good. It wrapped around my addled mind and comforted me. Told me that I was doing the right thing. That everything would be okay in the end.

I turned to face you. Saw the fear return to your eyes. And this time it wasn't the fear of what I had done, but of what I might do next.

You were right to be afraid.

I placed my hands on your shoulders. Not tightly, but I felt the tremble in you. Saw the tell-tale twitch at the corner of your eyes. You were going to cry.

'Do it!' shouted Flat Thirteen. Suddenly, her voice was accompanied by the thudding bass-line of rattled chains; the sounds of wriggling evil being spat out the end of a vacuum cleaner and into the world.

I screwed up my eyes, tightened my grip.

'Don't,' you said.

I did. I felt the release as you shattered the glass. Most of it fell out in one piece after you as you fell into the welcoming grasp of the dark water.

You bobbed to the surface once. I saw your bedraggled hair and your Edvard Munch face. But I never heard the scream.

After the police had gone and the storm had passed, I went back to the elevator. I'd ordered flowers on delivery and they'd come within just a couple of hours. I flung the fake flowers to the floor and re-placed them with real ones. I will do this every three or four days for the rest of my time here. I'm just sorry you had to get wrapped up in it all. It was nothing to do with you, I know that now.

Flat Thirteen is pleased with me. When the noises start now, it's not the disgruntled rattling of chains or the desperate voices. This time it kinda sounds like purring. The purring seems to vibrate through the wooden floors and off the panoramic window. It keeps me warm when I work late into the night. Sometimes, I reach out and try to make contact with the vibrations, so I can be less lonely. But they always seem to elude me.

Soon, I'm told, I will have to give the keys to Flat Thirteen back. Ap-parently, the recession's nearly over and people are willing to pay through the nose for places like this again. Only the other day a nice little family came to have a look around. The husband seemed very taken with the place. The wife told me that it looked like the kind of place she could picture herself writing her novel. Apparently, she becomes pretty obsessed when she starts to write.

Freak of Nature

by Richard Evans

Earth rise.

"Is it still beautiful, Doctor?"

The question takes its time to make sense in my brain. Earth hangs in black space, the blue marble. Near yet far. A world in turmoil, just like my own. I sigh. If I look straight ahead, grey terrain stretches out before me. Rocks and dust as far I can see. What did the voice clip at the Tranquillity Archive call it? A magnificent desolation. To the right are the ducts and domes of JAXA's Helium-3 plant, working day and night to keep us alive. Its egg shell power pods, white as Hokkaido snow when first constructed, are now streaked with the grey powder that gets everywhere. Everywhere. Maybe that's what's getting to us all. In the dim interior glow of the clinic, I can make out my reflection in the toughened glass. I look pale, a ghost captured in fragments of light.

"Earth rise, Doctor Kato." A calm voice reminds me of my train of thought. "You once said it was your favourite sight."

I turn. Sweep my hair into a ponytail. My skin feels like something sticky is clinging to it. I want to disappear into the shower for about an hour. Or two. Wash this place right off me.

"Nothing is beautiful at the moment." I speak through the protective barrier of a face mask lined with filters that monitor my every breath.

Ren is perfectly still in the clamshell recharging chair that is moulded like a second skin around him, his expression calm as he absorbs the He-3 that gives him life. For a moment, I wonder if he is here at all until his smooth carapace ripples, burnished like a pebble after years in the ocean. He finds me with almond eyes that are large and dark. I cannot hear a sound from his servos. We are as old as each other, yet I am the only one who feels the three decades that we have each been alive.

"I'm getting tired more often. I think my fuel cell is compromised."

"At least you have the chair—it'll have to do until things get back to normal."

In the background, snatches of radio chatter are exchanged between a passing freighter and the ground station seventy-five clicks down range. The crews seem to be sharing a joke. What can be so funny?

"You must be tired too, Doctor, you should have gone to bed hours ago. Go and get some sleep—I'll call you if there's an emergency." There is a soft hiss as he disconnects from the chair and stands up. He is a silhouette, quick and silent in the subdued glow from machines set into the hexagonal walls. He lifts a silicone-coated hand to my shoulder, my skin caressed as if by a butterfly's wing. It is a momentary relief. Behind the mask, I smile.

"I haven't seen you do that in a long time . . . " a pause, "Mai."

"You haven't said my first name in a long time either."

"Go to bed." His hand squeezes mine. "I will watch her."

"Are you sure? I'm her mother . . . "

"Yes, but she calls me 'Papa'."

He leans over the crib that sits beneath the window. Inside, Aiko lies still inside a clear antiseptic shield that covers and monitors her tiny body. Readouts flicker across the shield; blood pressure, heart rate, pulse . . . signs of life. Her chest lifts with light breaths. Two years old now, she is one of the first born here. I hate to see her wired like this. I blow a kiss at the crib then flee to my room before the tears can show.

A shot of TranQuil sends me under. Sleep can't come quickly enough. Just wish my dreams weren't so narcotic.

I am running. Falling. Legs are like dead weights that have no strength and make no headway. Like wading through treacle. Behind me is a mob, they cry and scream and chase. Somehow, I'm trying to run across a vast tract of space and getting nowhere fast. I have a mission to complete, a task too dreadful to fulfil. Earth is just out of reach and the mob is closing fast . . .

I'm woken by a beeping. A shrill tone that spares me from a desperate fate. Stumble like a drunk from foldout bunk to compact bathroom where I squint under brutal fluorescence. Find the sink, throw cold water on my face and in my eyes. Head feels worse than it did before I went to bed. The beeping grows louder. I know it's the phone but I don't want to talk. To anyone

A sigh as I find the handset and click accept.

"Doctor Kato?" The voice in the earpiece is crisp.

I close my eyes and search for strength. "Yes."

A sigh and then I activate the video feed—a screen unfolds from the handset like the petals of a spring flower. A bald head shines on the display, the caller's face lit by the gleam of Technate One's yin-yang logo.

"You know what time it is, Suarez?"

"Did I wake you? I'm sorry, I can never figure out lunar time. I just wanted to check on Aiko. How's she doing?"

"How d'you think?"

"You sound annoyed."

"I see you're feeling perceptive."

"Do you know why I'm calling?"

"Yes, but I don't know why I bothered answering."

"Our biomedics can help Aiko. Help all of you. And all we need is for you to bring her back to Earth."

"Sure. So you can patent a cure and then sell it back to us at a price we can't afford—just like you did with the nano-virus in Hong Kong and the Marburg mutations in Eastern Europe."

"Those were fair exchanges. Viral cultures for energy and food." He sniffs. "What you have up there could be interstellar in origin. It's a rare opportunity."

"I can't believe you just called the thing that's killed 68 people here an 'opportunity'."

He doesn't bat an eyelid. "All I mean is that what's hurting your people could be from a comet, or something long buried in one of the mines. Something from the beginning of the solar system itself. For the sake of all of us—not just your people—we need to understand what it is."

"And if you find an antidote to the Corona virus, how much will it cost us?"

A smile cracks his face. "The Technate is always happy to negotiate. There's sure to be something the colony can offer us."

"Yeah? What are you after? A better deal on Helium-3?"

"We just want to help."

"Go to hell, Suarez."

"I'm already there, honey. Two ex-wives and an ulcer the size of an old silver dollar."

"You'll get no sympathy from me."

"I'm not asking for it. Just reminding you that we're here for you—and your daughter. How many did you say the virus has taken now?"

"68."

"So that leaves . . . "

"26 of us." I cut him off. "Eight are showing signs and are in the clin-ic. The rest are managing to keep the mine running."

"And you have food? Water?"

"Enough for now."

"And how long since Aiko was diagnosed?"

"Three days."

He slips into silence, not blinking. Just the sound of his breath for a few moments. "There's still time. At least beam us her condition report. Our people can work on it from here."

"Even if I wanted to send her to you, I couldn't. You're forgetting the small matter of our quarantine status. Earth doesn't want us, only the Helium-3."

"I can arrange safe passage for Aiko. We have a medical ship in lunar orbit, it can be with you in a few hours."

"And that will be enough to get through Disease Control?"

"We think that putting her in ColdStor will halt the spread of the virus."

"How many will this ship of yours carry?"

He hold up his hand, makes a fist then extends two fingers. "Room for a child and her mother."

"And what would happen to me? A prison term for breaching quarantine?"

"Sometimes a parent must make sacrifices for her child."

"And what about Ren?"

Suarez struggles to control a smirk. "Sorry. Just room for two."

"I'm surprised you don't want to just leave us here to die—then there won't be anything between you and the isotope mines."

"You're getting paranoid up there, Mai. Stir crazy." He shakes his head. "Just think about it, will you? But not for too long. Aiko doesn't have that luxury."

I throw the handset at the wall and stumble back to the bathroom.

In the airlock at the clinic's entrance, I don a face mask detailed with a hand-stitched Murakami logo, custom-made in the Gion Urbanate and a reminder of home. Enzymes woven into the fabric search for signs of infection and I hold my breath until the strap-mounted LED glows green. The clinic doors hiss and slide apart.

Ren is leaning down by the crib, reciting a story to Aiko, playing sound effects to complement the tale. If she can hear him, she shows no sign of responding.

"What are you reading to her?"

"The Peach Boy."

"Oh, I used to love that that story when I was little."

"I know, that's why I chose it."

"So how is she?"

"Beautiful." He stands up, elegant and sleek. "But she is frail. She seems to be fighting but I don't know if she can win."

Aiko is bathed in a therapeutic golden glow, tubes in her button nose and a drip strapped to her left arm. Thick dark hair is lank on her pillow. Her favourite toy, Panda Bear, lies next to her patiently keeping her company. Her breath is accompanied by a rhythmic sequence of lights and beeps from the rack of machines in the wall above her crib. All around her mouth and nose is a telltale white ooze, Corona's cruel signature. It is the same for the eight crew members sealed in the adult beds next door, each trapped in the cocoon that the disease wraps around them.

Ren uses his index finger to draw a display on the wall. It lights up with real-time charts showing Aiko's deteriorating condition.

"It's eating away at her immune and respiratory systems—trying to weaken her before a full-on attack. Turning her body against her at a cellular level. I've removed the protein repressors but it's just not working. Her genomic sequence is good—she's a strong child but . . . " he seems lost in the data-glow from the screen, "I've never seen a pathogen as resilient as this."

"And we still have no idea where it came from."

He shrugs. "Microbial life has survived intolerable conditions on Mars. Could have gotten here on a cargo vessel. Or maybe we dug it up with the Helium-3. Who knows?"

My hands are clasped in front of me, as if in prayer. "I wish I could hold her."

"The machines are caring for her now. We're doing everything possible." Ren takes my left hand. "Have you slept?"

I shake my head. "A little."

"You need to keep your strength. Let's get you some food."

"But one of us should stay -"

"It's ok. I'll get a message if there is the slightest change."

He guides me out to the automat across the corridor. I push buttons on the bank of vending machines, wait for food and drink to be dispensed, then select one of many empty booths. The seats are lined with white faux-leather. Ren and I are alone beneath a liquid crystal glow,

I play with a piece of toast and sip at a cup of green tea. Classical music is discreet through hidden speakers. Bach's Goldberg Variations.

"So I had a call from Suarez."

"I was wondering when you were going to tell me."

His eyes are intense and I shrink beneath his gaze.

"I forgot you knew."

"They made me so that I see everything that goes on here." He taps his head; silicone on composite polymers.

"He wants me to take Aiko back to Earth. Says he can get her treatment."

"They'll never let her through. She's too contagious."

"He says they can freeze the virus by putting her in ColdStor."

I push myself along the seat closer to Ren and he wraps his arms around me, then kisses my cheek with tender lips. I close my eyes.

"If the virus reaches Earth, it could obliterate them. That's too big a risk to save just one child." Tears well and I dab my cheek. The green tea grows cold in the white ceramic cup, its flavour fading. "But I'm her mother— I'm supposed to protect her. She's done nothing to deserve this."

"What's happening here does not make you a bad mother," he strokes my hair with a warm hand, whispering to me, "it is out of everybody's control."

Our eyes meet. Mine tearful, his almost compassionate.

"I think they want us all to die."

"Then I would be without you," his voice is plaintive, "in this barren place."

"Don't say that. Don't say that, Ren. We're a family and I won't leave you here."

The walkway from the automat to the prayer module is long and takes me beyond the media suite, the nursery and the gymnasium. The tube is softened angles, white walls and a subdued glow from the solar cells. Mementoes of humankind's trips to the moon, images of Apollo and Zarya, Polaris and Vega, the faces of long-dead astronauts honoured in sacred silence, captured behind glass in their moment of making history. The photographs used to inspire me but lately, they just make me sad.

A sensor reads the chip in my arm and lets me into the module, another hexagon where tatami mats cover the floor and a torii gate takes centre stage. The wooden monolith has a shimenawa hanging from its crossbeam. The room has one large window that offers a panoramic view of the Peary Crater, where our outpost clings on a peak of eternal light. A stream of water flows through stones at the base of the shrine, so I light an incense stick and bow down in prayer to the kami and to my ancestors. The aroma of sandalwood fills the room and with all my heart, I wish that I could hold Aiko, pick her up and see her smile once more. Tears flow and my body aches from a cut that has not yet been made.

W hen the tears subside, I find myself staring out of the window at the crater. The peaks of its jagged rim forged long ago by lava spewed from a violent impact. Light cannot enter there and the darkness never escapes. The Moon is still and silent and ancient, a remnant of the moment before the beginning of time.

The door to the module slides open behind me.

A pause, then—"do you mind if I come in?"

I smile to myself. "You are always so polite, even after all this time." I wave Ren over to my side. "Of course you can come in here."

"This another of your favourite views?"

I take a breath before answering. "The only things that move out there are the shadows."

"I'd like to take a walk outside—all the way to that peak." He points to a summit nearly twenty kilometres distant.

"One fine day, when we're free of Corona and the supply ships come again, they'll bring you a new fuel cell and you'll be able to go wherever you want without needing your recharge chair every few hours."

"I feel like a prisoner here."

"You're not alone with that."

His gaze stays fixed on the rim of the crater. I take his hand in mine. "When this is over, I'll go out there with you. I promise."

R en is in shadow, framed by the light from Aiko's crib. Shape-memory muscles flex beneath clear silicone skin as he rests graceful hands on narrow hips.

"You seen it?"

"What?"

He nods at light moving across a screen set into the clinic's wall. "Telemetry says it's a Technate shuttle, direct from the NuMex spaceport."

"Suarez doesn't give up, does he?"

He shrugs. "It's a drone." He stands straight and fixes me with dark eyes. "You said it was coming."

"Like I told you, Suarez wants me to go back with Aiko."

"Is that what you want?"

For the first time I can remember, his voice is cold.

"Oh Ren. Of course not."

His stare is unreadable for a minute until his shoulders sag. Thin fingers rub his smooth forehead, as if frustrated. "I'm sorry. I was worried." He smiles, contrite. "I understand that you will want to go. That Aiko comes before me . . . "

"But we're a family and what I want is that the three of us stay here. Always."

"Yes, but Aiko is sick . . . "

"All that the Technate wants is the virus. Saving her life is a side issue to them."

" . . . and you're her mother, it is right that you'll do anything to save her." Eyes on the floor now. "And I am here to help you."

I cross the room to where he stands. He is statuesque in the soft light. I smile and pull him towards me. "Come on, there's nothing for us to argue about."

For a few moments, he just stares without responding.

My hand on his arm. "Sometimes Ren, I have no idea what you're thinking."

His hands move from his side, one to my neck and the other fumbles under my thin shirt. Hips press. I moan. Stroke him as we kiss. Feel his hand in my hair, his fingers caressing the back of my neck. His hand moves quickly around my throat. Tightening.

"Ren . . . " I gasp, "you're hurting me." I push against him but he won't let go, doesn't react to my cries. "What are you doing?"

My fingers grow numb and the clinic and Ren and Aiko tumble. As air diminishes, panic rises. I have no strength to fight, He is too strong, too focused. Tears fill my eyes. His gaze is intense as the light fades.

"I'm sorry . . . "

Are the last words I hear.

Out of the vacuum, air. Out of the blackness, a blur of blue and gold. There is a voice, a mouth. It moves but it may as well be speaking in tongues. Bright light hurts my eyes, but I don't close them. For a long time, I simply stare.

My throat hurts. Panic! Adrenalin kicks and I sit up, poised for another attack. Precious air fills my lungs. I can breathe. The space is cramped, silent. I am not alone.

"Aiko!"

Straps criss-cross my body and hold me tight on a single couch. Across the cabin, Aiko's cot is lodged beneath a single blue light. She is pale and still. ColdStor. Text and charts flicker across the plastic shield that protects her, constant updates that let me know she is alive.

A screen above my head blinks and unfolds with a soft chime. Ren's smooth face fills the small display

"Are you ok, Mai?"

"What did you do to me? What's going on?"

"I'm so sorry. I hope I didn't hurt you too much. The marks on your neck will disappear in a day or two."

"You choked—did you choke me?"

"It was the only way.

"The only way to do what?"

He steps back, the lens that captures him wobbles and his image judders on my screen. The backdrop is grey dust and black sky. Behind him is a sealed airlock.

Realisation hits like a cold ocean wave.

"You put me on the shuttle." Another rush of panic. "Aiko too."

"It was the only way." He repeats.

"Ren, what have you done? I told you they only want to exploit her."

"At least this way she has a chance to live."

"Please tell me you're not outside the station."

Alloys flex his face into a weak smile.

"Get back in. Now."

He shakes his head. "I want to see the view from the peak of the mountain."

"But you won't make it—your fuel cell won't last."

"Mai, this way she has a chance. It is the right thing to do."

"Please Ren. Go back inside and let me turn this ship around."

"It's on an auto-return trajectory to NuMex. You'll be out of quarantine in six months—sooner, once they know you're not infected." The screen blanks for a moment, then Ren's face reappears. He is walking now. "In a minute, I'll have gone too far to turn round." His expression drops. "I never imagined that I would be here without you and Aiko."

My throat aches and tears pour down my cheeks.

"Don't cry, Mai. I'm so sorry for what I did to you. I couldn't think of another way." Rhythmic snatches of static interrupt the signal like the slow beating of a drum. "You'll be out of range in a few seconds, once you cross to the far side." His attention drifts and his eyes grow wide and the image fragments.

"Ren, no!"

"I never knew there were so many stars."

CABALA

The static beats to a white noise roll and then—
Blank screen.

Bird-Girl of Belomorsk

by Rachel Kendall

In the frozen white plains of Belomorsk, Russia, there is said to be a small yet magnificent castle. Circling its walls like a wreath is the forest, enchanted they say, with trees so tall they cast shadows on even the tallest of the castle's tall towers. In this castle lives a prince, heir to the throne and top marksman to the king. It is said he is reclusive, and slightly mad, spending all his time hunting the rare and the strange. A well-travelled man, the prince has trophies of his kills on display, and a curious public will pay vast monies just to take a peek of such beauties as the Moravian tigersnake and the lesserspotted multi-hued dormouse of Damascus.

One clear day, when he was out hunting, the prince heard a beautiful and unusual sound. This was neither lark nor nightingale song, but the musical charms of a siren and he felt drawn to its magic. He tipped the barrel of his gun, rested the butt on his shoulder and walked toward the sound. It was a peculiar bird he saw, sitting pretty on the branch of a gnarly old tree. Blacker than midnight she was, with a glint of pink wing-tip and a bloody red beak. The prince had never seen such a fine specimen. He could picture this beautiful trophy stuffed and mounted beside the albino gorilla paw in his antechamber. Dr von Blerring, the taxidermist, might fill her with magic beans and stitch her up in fine spun thread. His heart thumped with excitement at the thought. And then perhaps he could woo the charming Lady Rebecca into marriage. He aimed his gun at the delicate warbling throat and pulled the trigger.

After the gunshot came silence.

And then the desperate guttural sounds of distress could be heard from a few feet away. She wasn't dead. The king's top marksman had missed his target. The shame would be unbearable. Anger washed over his body in pinpricks and his cheeks and throat flushed scarlet beneath the black stubble. Muttering under his breath he took heavy, grass-flattening strides towards the sound.

What he saw melted his anger in a cloud. Pity, he felt. And awe and disgust. The black and pink bird was no longer a bird but a woman, with the breasts and hips of a woman, with sea-salt pink flesh and black feathers for hair. Her waist was tapered like an insect's and in the soft round belly her naval was so deep the prince had to resist peering into it for fear of losing his soul. She was crying but shedding no tears. She only made that sound, that insistent, persistent wail from her pursed red lips, that sent a chill through to the prince's very bones. Her arm bled, the blood thick and drip-dropping as insistently as her cry. But her thighs were creamy pink smooth and he had to resist the urge to place one small fingertip on the skin to see if she were as smooth as she looked. And then she wriggled. She sat up and looked at him, pulled her feet from beneath her, and lo!—he saw she had a pair of leathery black bird's feet instead of ten human toes. The skin was stretched tight and parched and the claws were two inches long. Three toes facing forward on each foot and one to the back, but it seemed these feet were useless. They hung limp like tanned hide, the clawed tips slightly curled. Around one ankle, a silver ring, inscribed with the cursive script of some code or magic spell, dug deep into the flesh where woman skin met that of the bird she used to be. The prince shed a few tears for her then, touched to his heart by the revolting sight of this creature, and she sat still and let him hold her close to his chest. Then, with a heavy sigh, he swept her up into his arms and carried her back to the castle.

"What is your name?" he asked as the nurse busied herself in tending to the blood. The bullet had barely grazed the girl's arm and the wound was not nearly as bad as it had looked.

"Are you shy?" He placed his finger beneath her chin to bring her gaze to his, but she struggled and looked away. "Can't you talk?"

She hadn't stopped whimpering, though he knew she was not in any pain for the nurse had administered drugs to ease her. What a shame she couldn't give her something for the noise too.

And so she came to live with the prince. Her wound healed and she gained the strength back in her feet. She couldn't walk like any normal woman, but she could manoeuvre herself from one room to the next. She even managed to get up the spiral staircase where he would find her staring pitifully out of the tiny window of the tallest tower. The prince hated to see her creeping around and would carry her whenever he could. Her movements were monstrous, crippling, and it disgusted him. He let her share his bed, the comfort of silk sheets and velvet cushions, but she would lie on its very edge and sob. She wouldn't open to him at all. Like a stone she was. Hard and cold. So he left her to the tower. But once when she was found limping out of the front door he had to take drastic action and took to shackling her wrists and ankles to prevent her escape. She wasn't a prisoner, but neither was she capable of living freely in the forest in this new form of hers. She wouldn't survive a night. So to save her being savaged by dogs or freezing to death, this was the way it had to be. A new ring. A new owner. He couldn't remove the evidence of a previous possession. He had tried everything, had mortified her flesh with pincers and knives as he attempted to saw through the metal. But it wouldn't give and her blood had stained his good carpet.

Time passed. She refused to speak. She was a thousand voices but each one was like that of a sinner in purgatory. It hurt his head to hear her. The feathers in her hair began to fall and lay like leaves on the floor. Her lips lost their crimson hue and turned a purple blue, and her eyes became clouded in pink. She refused to eat the chunks of soft white bread he broke off for her, and she let his red wine pour from her open mouth. Sometimes she spat it back at him, leaving a bloody red stain on his skin as he had on hers. In the end he had no choice but to bring her grubs and insects to eat after he caught her eyeing the fleshy brown body of a spider, and dirty rain water collected from the puddles outside. She was dying. He knew that. She had become a pathetic and diluted version of her former bird-self. She had become like one of the dirty town birds the prince had seen on occasion. Those with decaying black stumps for feet and feathers tarred in shit. There was no choice but to renew her beauty. To give her the splendour he had originally intended to bestow. So one night, when she was sleeping, head lolling and a string of drool spotting her naked breast he crept up behind her. In a single swoop he grabbed what was left of her hair and sliced her from ear to ear.

There was once a Russian prince, the king's top marksman, who collected his prey like trophies. He and his wife, the consumptive Princess Rebecca, opened their castle doors to the paying public. Day after day the insatiable crowd would walk the dark corridors of this morbid museum and stop in wonder at the very last exhibit. For there, behind glass, was a most magnificent specimen. A creature, with the full-fleshed body of a woman, but the black withered feet of a bird. She had the most luscious red lips, the brightest pink eyes and a mane of long black feathers. A straight line from naval to breast shone in a criss-cross of bright gold stitching and her skin was pearl in contrast. Her head slightly lowered, her swan-like neck hidden, and her lips pursed as though holding a silent note. Around one ankle, a silver ring, and beneath this a plaque that simply read—Bird-girl of Belomorsk.

Son of a Preacherman

by A.J Kirby

Hedley stared hard at his son and willed him not to wake up. Although the boy was clearly well into the REM stage, Hedley was painfully aware of how light a sleeper he was. He seemed sensitive to even the most subtle movement; magically attuned to even the gentle eddies of thought which reverberated out from other people. He'd have made a good watch-dog.

And so, big old Hedley had learned to become a statue. He'd trained his body to become part of the furniture. When the cramps set in, and he had to shift his weight on the chair, he did it in stages, so as to avoid any creaks. He regulated his breathing and took great care not to give in to the unpredictability which had formerly governed his bulky frame. And he was surprised to find that he was good at it; he was good at being a non-person.

The room was thick with the smell of talcum power and the sweet, almost imperceptible odour of Joseph's boyish sweat. Like every night, Hedley's hands were clenched together, fingers entwined, either in prayer or as a simple, primal gesture of hope.

'Please God, let him sleep through. Let us not enter into any fresh hell tonight,' he breathed, softly, fearful that even the merest whisper could rouse him.

Hedley was nearly made to regret his rash words. Even at their almost inaudible volume, they'd done something. Joseph's brow suddenly creased, he murmured looked as though he was going to open his eyes, but then he settled back into the turgid goose-feather pillow and resumed his metronomic breathing.

The momentary panic over, Hedley regarded his son. He had a button-nose, fine pink lips and piercing blue eyes, just like his father. Oh yes,

Joseph was a beautiful boy, of that there was no doubt, but recently he'd been showing signs of fatigue beyond his years. When he was awake, worry-lines ran across his forehead. Only when he was asleep could Hedley see him as he wanted to, as the innocent that he was, free from burden.

Hedley watched him and watched him, leaning forward to the edge of his chair as though to monitor the progress of each and every breath. His vigilance brought him a feeling of great responsibility. This little man before him could do anything, be anyone, but in these stolen moments, he was still only his father's son, and as such, still relied upon him for guidance and protection, for wisdom and advice.

But there was confusion in Hedley's eyes as well as pride. He looked as though he was waiting to learn some important truth from his son's sleeping form. Perhaps the night-time visits were a result of a yearning for everything to be as it once was. In those moments, perhaps Hedley could still picture himself as the kind of father that he'd always wanted to be. Perhaps he could still picture himself as the kind of father he wanted to be: one-part climbing frame, one-part story book, one-part clown. Perhaps he thought HE could still stand guard by the bed and prevent the avarice and falsity of the world from touching his son until he was old enough to understand it a little better. But it was long past that point, wasn't it?

Hedley shifted uncomfortably in the chair and listened to the insistent ticking of the clock. His hand escaped, once, to rub some life back into his tiring eyes. But he didn't sleep. He didn't sleep despite the dark pools which lay underneath them, despite the fact that his eyelids had puffed out so much that they now looked like over-cooked conchiglie. They were extravagantly red-rimmed. Since Sally left, Hedley had become nostalgic for a past that he'd hardly even noticed when he was living it. He'd become wistful and teary-eyed at the most inopportune moments—in the middle of sermons for instance. Now they wheeled him out only in the direst of need. They had people that were far hungrier for success than him, people who had far fewer personal issues. Hedley was falling apart, and he knew it.

Joseph moved again. As though reacting to some unnoticed draft, he wrapped himself more tightly within the thick blue duvet, but still, one naked leg, always that one leg, extended outwards and out of the stifling thing. As he settled back down, a lock of yellow hair flopped in front of his eyes. Hedley longed to reach out and push it away with his thumb, but knew that to allow himself such a simple, brief pleasure would be sinfully negligent of the long-term consequences.

Joseph's shockingly blonde hair had long-since become one of those minefields that every family has. He was growing it long, on the advice of Solomon, but that meant that it tufted up like bulrushes when it was pressed sweatily against the pillows during the night. In the morning, it would take some hard tugs of the comb, punctuated by shrieking complaints on the boy's part, to drag them back into place. Hedley wished that he was able to make his own decisions regarding the boy's hairstyle.

Sighing, Hedley closed his eyes, shook his head a moment as though dispensing with some troublesome thought, and then opened them again. He looked surprised to be in the bedroom. He looked, dare one say it, disappointed to be there. To be fair to Hedley, Joseph's bedroom was particularly sparsely decorated. It was so bare that it almost resembled a monastic cell or perhaps, more accurately a half-finished hotel room, complete with the red-leather covered bible on the bedside table. Hedley had once tried to add a little colour to the room, but Joseph had become agitated and had cried a Noah's flood of tears, and the decorations had to go. He liked it just the way it was.

Once again, a muffled sound emanated from under the bedclothes. Once again, Hedley immediately became alert, sat up straight-backed in the chair and waited. This time, however, there was to be no escape, for to his horror Joseph then opened his eyes.

'I had a dream,' said Joseph in a voice still muffled by sleep.

Hedley sighed impatiently.

'Don't you want to hear about my dream, father? You used to love to hear about my dreams,' continued Joseph, puffing up his pillows and sitting up in bed.

'And what did you dream about Joseph?' asked Hedley, attentively now. He seemed nervous somehow.

'I dreamed that I was walking in the desert and there was nothing around for miles. I was lonely and hungry and thirsty and tired and I thought that I couldn't go on. I wanted to give in to temptation and lie on down and be feeble. There wasn't even plants there, father, nor trees or beasts. It was like God had called forth a gigantic sandstorm to cover the earth and I was the only one left. I was ever so lonesome. But I heard a voice. A deep, lovely voice like Solomon's at Church, but different. Of course, I knew who that voice might be and I felt mighty relieved and comforted to hear it. I wasn't on my own in that big-massive desert any more. And that voice talked to me and it told me that I must follow the one true path if we are all to be saved. It told me that we must shun the temptations of the devil and we must not listen to the false preachings of the internet. It told me that I must pass my message on to the followers, father, just like it did before.'

Hedley looked down at his son with sadness in his eyes. 'The voice says that we can't have the computer now?' he asked, softly. 'As well as the television and the radio? Are you sure that's what it wanted?'

'Why yes, father. Do you doubt me?' asked Joseph, narrowing his eyes menacingly.

'Of course not, Joseph,' said Hedley, rather too quickly. 'Do you want me to write it down before you forget?'

Hedley jumped to his feet and crossed the room. He pulled out a thick spiral-bound notepad from the desk drawer, selected a biro rather than a fountain pen, and returned to his seat.

'I won't forget because Jesus' words stay imprinted on the brain. Solomon told me,' snapped Joseph, rubbing the last remnants of sleep from his eyes.

Hedley bent over his notebook and scrawled while Joseph repeated his telling of the dream. On a couple of occasions where the story deviated particularly wildly from the original telling—the introduction of a faithful dog at one point, for instance—Hedley raised his eyebrows, but he said nothing, simply continued to note down his son's words.

'And that's everything?' he asked, finally.

'Yup. I think I'll go back to sleep now.'

Hedley knew that he wouldn't be getting any sleep that night. He had arrangements to make, publicity to organise, deals to broker. He had to speak to Solomon. As he slunk out of Joseph's room, a look of thunder clouded his face.

Hedley nursed his steaming cup of coffee and waited for Solomon to deign to call him back. These days, it was difficult for him to remember how wonderful it had felt to be a part of something so big. When he'd been initiated into the inner-circle, he'd felt as though the whole world was at his feet; they'd shown him marvellous things, let him in on wondrous secrets. They'd asked him to spread the word, once. But he'd become disillusioned, hadn't he? Not so much that he'd stopped believing, but enough that they stopped trusting him so readily to be their enthusiastic voice from the altar. And then Solomon had somehow heard about the young Joseph. He'd shown signs of being a good orator even in Sunday School, and when he'd started with the dreams too, Solomon thought all his Sundays had come at once. He'd begun to groom him, making him the sorcerer's apprentice. And of course, the people had loved him too. Word of his dreams spread like wild-fire.

But then the demands for more and more had come in: the touring, the constant desire for new dreams, new messages. Both Hedley and Joseph had found it difficult to cope. Sally had simply left.

'This isn't what a young boy should be doing,' she said on that fateful night in their kitchen. 'You're subjecting him to the ridicule of the world at too early an age. I think he's just making these dreams up just to satisfy the demand. Look at the way that you sit by his bed, pen in hand, waiting for the next "message from beyond".'

Young Joseph was hiding between Hedley's great tree-trunk legs, hiding from his mother's watchful eye. Hedley couldn't allow such wild accusations to simply hang there in the air, could he?

'And you're an unbeliever. You're trying to make us doubt,' he said. 'You aren't a suitable influence for our son.'

Of course, Sally had begged Joseph to go with her, but the young lad was just about as stubborn as Hedley, even then, and he'd hung back between his father's legs and made his choice. Sometimes Hedley wished that Joseph had made a different choice now—the purer choice.

The church was set up as though in preparation for the visit of the Pope. There were vast metal barriers flanking the entire road leading up to the entrance, posters adorned the walls, the not-so-subtle presence of the police in case the crowd got out of hand. Inside, microphones and sound systems had been set up, startled-looking roadies ferried large amplifiers to the back of the stage and the inner-circle rushed around rectifying flower arrangements. The atmosphere was heavy with anticipation. Everyone was pinning their hopes on the small boy with the sandy hair.

Hedley and Joseph were sipping scalding tea from a cauldron-like urn in the large but deserted room adjacent to the stage. They were trying to ignore the chants of the crowd outside which wafted in through the open windows, trying to pretend that this was just a day in church, like any other. They were trying to drown out the frenzied baying of the mob with polite small-talk.

'I thought we might go for a walk in the park after this,' said Hedley.

'I don't like the park. It is a haven for the fallen. Solomon says so.'

The father in Hedley longed to reach out to this fragile boy, who was trying to wear a mask of determination but who looked rather constipated by fear.

'Are you sure that you want to do this?' he asked. He spoke so softly that his voice could hardly be heard above the clamour.

'Course I am father,' said Joseph in that scary, monotone voice he seemed to have adopted for times like these.

'But . . . are you sure that you want to tell them about this particular dream?' continued Hedley.

'Why?' asked Joseph, with a gleam of something wicked in the corner of his eye.

'Well, you know that a lot of people could . . . well, could you not tell them something else?'

'Do you not believe the sanctity of the message?' said a voice from behind them. Hedley saw Joseph's face crack into a wide smile. It was the first proper sign of emotion he'd seen in his son for what felt like weeks. He spun in his seat to be greeted by the sight of Solomon, resplendent in the flowing robes he chose for each and every occasion which Joseph spoke.

Immediately, Solomon's presence dominated the room. He loomed over them, Hedley shrinking back into his seat.

'Well? Do you doubt your son's dream?' he asked again with that deep booming voice of his. There was an impression of great authority in his words, hypnotic power. Every word seemed interlaced with the message there can be no doubt. Hedley couldn't speak. He felt as though he was being buffeted by some powerful wind which at any moment could topple him over the precipice.

Suddenly, Solomon's stern face relaxed into a wonderful smile and he began to ruffle at Joseph's sandy hair.

'You're getting a fine mane these days, Brother Joseph,' he said, merrily, before flashing him that same smile again. It was the kind of smile that made you feel special if it shined its particular light on you, the very smile, in fact, that Hedley remembered so well from his own youth.

'Is your father's doubt holding you back, child?' said Solomon in a vaguely jocular manner. He held out a chocolate biscuit to the boy, as though it was a promise of things to come. 'Would you prefer to come and live with Brother Solomon?'

'I fear that he is becoming an unbeliever,' whispered Joseph, snatching at the chocolate biscuit and spiriting it away into some fold in his own robes. 'I fear that he is trying to cloud my visions.'

Hedley stared at his son with shock, his face sliding into grey confusion.

'Are you an unbeliever, Hedley?' asked Solomon, a more sinister tone creeping into his voice once more.

'No . . . I . . . I . . . It's not as simple as that.'

'Well, I'll ask you something simpler then. Do you believe that your son was really spoken to by God last night?'

Hedley's eyes wavered between the expectant eyes of his son and the malevolent sparkle of Solomon's eyes. He had no idea what he should say.

'Come on, Joseph; his silence speaks for itself,' said Solomon, at once leading the child through the adjoining door and onto the edge of the stage. A great roar erupted from the crowd.

'Joe . . . Joe . . . ' shouted Hedley, but his cries were futile. The crowd were in raptures now. Head in hands, he heard Solomon introducing his son, crowning him as the chosen one.

'He is a special boy; a messenger of God. But he is more than simply our channel to God, he is our interpreter. I'd like you to give a great North Western welcome to the one and only Joseph Serum.'

'Speak Truth, Serum! Speak Truth, Serum!' roared the crowd. But then, as the boy stepped forward, a reverential hush descended.

The young boy spoke with a zeal that reminded Hedley of Solomon. The crowd were magnetically attracted by his mixture of wisdom, insight and other-worldliness. Hedley felt himself drawn to the stage. He had to see what the others saw. He staggered to his feet and hid in the shadows at the side of the stage.

What Hedley saw almost killed him. His son was like a classically trained actor. His speech was laden with inflection, with weighty pauses and with gesture. He was magnificent. Despite everything, Hedley felt a surge of pride . . . until he felt the presence of Solomon at his shoulder.

'Remember the agreement you signed?' he hissed. 'You wanted to share everything with the Church. You thought that meant that you'd have access to the spoils of little Joe's preachings, did you? Well, it works the other way too. The church has access to everything you own.'

Hedley felt rough hands grabbing him. He felt himself being dragged away from the stage. Hedley Serum lost his son, and suddenly felt closer to God than he had in a long, long time.

The Fox and the No-Moon

by Rachel Kendall

Burned-out chariots glowed like fireflies and the sound of gunfire echoed through the forest. Trees felled themselves, creaking and crashing in despair, and the tides became knotted in their confusion of coming and going. Once again the moon had failed to show. Never before had she overslept like this. Some folk said she had fallen out with the sun and refused to play her part; others said she had a palsy and was too ashamed to show her withered face. Still others dared to say she had died. Just that. She had died and there was no heir to her throne.

And since her no-show, everything had changed. There was gang-warfare amongst the shoemaker's elves, the seven dwarves were on strike, Cinders had left her prince and run off with a pauper and Puss in Boots had been seen moonlighting in the strip club wearing nothing but red stilettos and a thong.

From high up in her room Poppy could see how the forest was losing the battle to keep the peace. The air smelled of sabotage, of blood and death and fire. It was scorched with gunpowder. The good were turning bad and the evil were becoming indifferent. The balance was lost. For Poppy it had become a kind of lethargy. A total loss of interest in life and the forest she once loved. She no longer left her tower, marrying herself instead to its quiet heights. She used to love the feel of grass beneath her bare feet, the scent of wildflowers and the song of the sea at the forest's edge. She had been full of passion, hot-blooded and a little wild. She had been known to sneak downstairs in the dead of night and dance under the silvery moon.

But she no longer danced. She barely moved from her bed to her desk where she read the local news on the internet rather than hearing it on the vine. And with this boredom came a quiet, smouldering anger. Two opposite emotions in resistance. She didn't care that the flowers were being trampled and left bloody from the slayings or that the constellations were being plucked from the sky one by one. She didn't care and she was angry that she didn't care. She was too angry and too bored to do anything about it. There was no pleasure to be found anywhere. Even her vibrator remained quiet as a mouse beneath her bed. Her bed which felt lumpy despite the nineteen golden-goose feather mattresses she slept on. She had spots appearing on her forehead and chin, and when she last looked in the mirror it had threatened to crack. It refused to tell her who was the fairest of them all, and spoke only of the recent spate in cosmic surgery.

Poppy blamed the no-moon. She had not bled for an age, neither the red of her gypsy mother nor the blue of her royal father. Her womb was restless, but lethargic. With no blood to lose and no new life to be made, the body it occupied was coming to the end of its vacuity tether. There are shallower and shallower pools and Poppy now paddled in waters barely deep enough to wet the soles of her feet, and she was even getting bored of the internet, PlayStation and Wii. She had no friends to chat to and no handsome prince to kiss. The only man she had ever known (for three days) and loved, Felix, had been banished from the kingdom. Simply for holding her hand.

She paced the room, throwing open her wardrobe doors to look at her beautiful dresses. Lace and silk and satin, retro and vintage in "green genie", "ruby Tuesday" and "hot pink". They bored her. What was the point of these beautiful things when she had nowhere to go?

She wriggled over to the window in her fish-tail ballgown and tippy-tapped her acrylic nails over the dust-covered lids of her jars and bottles of poisons. Her love of toxicology had left months ago. Her deadly plants and even her prickly pear had begun to droop. She had lost interest in her magic-making and now preferred image-faking, a kind of glamour without the need for a spell. Her reflection showed a beautiful young woman, slender and delicate, with skin the fake colour of mocha. Her blonde hair was thick and very, very long and shone like gold.

She sighed loudly. She was so *bored*.

Beast, her Peruvian hairless dog, lay asleep in his basket. He was no company. One-leg, the nightingale her father had wounded on one of his hunts and brought back to her as a gift, no longer bothered to sing. She used to do a fantastic Amy Winehouse set but these days she barely bothered to hum an Elvis medley. Everything was silent and closed because the whole forest had forgotten its charms. The mussels by the sea remained shut, the oysters refused to yield, the clams clammed and the flowers in the forest budded tight in their skull caps. Even during the day the sun seemed to shine less as though he missed his sombre friend. He cast a dull yellow as far as the eye could see and the people of the village longed for the dramatic shapes the moon had once cast, the chiaroscuro of distorted figures she created, a whole world of Medusa-style artwork from Land's Beginning to Land's End. But not any more.

The sound of a gun shot nearby woke Poppy from her reverie. Granny. She must have caught another one. The gingerbread granny-flat Poppy's dad had erected sure did bring in the food, though only granny ate children. The rest of the family settled for wild boar and homing pigeon.

" . . . teach you to go sniffing around my chickens," her voice screeched through the night like a banshee.

Something was happening. And the fact that something rather than nothing was happening was certainly something to be curious about. Poppy kicked off her Christian Louboutin glass slippers and paced the room. Never had she felt so trapped. Since the moon had disappeared her father had installed Tweedledo and Tweedledon't at the foot of her tower, "for her own protection". But she knew they were the fat fleshy equivalent of a chastity belt. Which meant her father didn't trust her, thought she was still a child, didn't want her to be touched, looked at, breathed upon. As though she weren't already spoiled goods from under-use. She stormed over to her bedside table where Warren, a miniature giant, sat atop his bonsai beanstalk, practicing his fee fi fo fums. With a quick flick of her finger and thumb she sent him flying through the air. He landed on her bed with a grunt, slightly winded but otherwise unhurt. He was used to her tantrums and mischief. She watched as he struggled in the sea of her bedspread before deftly fashioning himself a silken rope and descending to the floor.

"Holy fuck, Warren, you're a genius!" This princess was no lady, you see, her grammar and choice of language were instrumental in creating the vocal interpretation of a soiled pair of disposable briefs. But she had been inspired and it was a whole new experience. In intellect she had chosen the short straw, but in looks she more than made up for it. She did have other qualities too, once. Some have said she was kind. That she was a tender and loving child who kept gerbils, hamsters, mice, pygmy dragons and other caged vermin. But the long years of solitude and lack of fresh air had taken their toll. Since the hunting accident that had killed her mother, she had been spoiled and turned rotten. She had become a sour, lonely and bored young woman with her own tanning salon and a laptop to match every outfit. And things had only got worse since the time of the no-moon.

She grabbed hold of her hair extensions and yanked as hard as she could. Out they came, with a bloody rip of her scalp, but she barely felt the pain for the anticipation of leaving the tower. Fixing one end of the hair to the windowsill she gingerly heaved herself over, catching her dress on a nail and tearing it a gaping wound. She began her frightening descent amidst the hollow sound of the forest at war, and a bullet ricocheted inches from her nose. She hurried faster, faster down the tower. As she moved her body swung to and fro, banging against the ivory, bruising her elbows and scraping her knees. Her false nails snapped off one after the other leaving her fingers looking stumpy and pale. And then she was at the bottom, struggling to defend herself against the particularly nasty beetle-thorn shrub she had planted herself as a child.

That was when she felt something warm and wet circle her wrist. A bite so gentle that not a single incisor pierced her. She felt herself being pulled free of the shrub and as she came into the clearing, the moon freed herself from the gnarly grey fingers of a tangle-cloud and lit up clearly the bloody, bruised woman and the fox that had saved her.

"What the—? What are you doing? Granny'll *kill* you. She shoots foxes."

"I had to see you," he said. He spoke just like a man and his yellow eyes were kind and full of compassion. "I don't know why, exactly. I've been waiting outside this tower for so long, trying to figure out how to get up to you."

"Are you here to rescue me?"

He frowned and the black tips of his ears drooped. "I don't know."

More shots sounded, closer than before. Had granny come out of hiding? Had she overcome her fear of the fairy folk in order to have her kill tonight? She hated foxes more than she hated children. She would rip out their claws and poke out their eyes before boiling them alive. The children she would at least kill first, before tenderising, seasoning, and serving with relish.

Poppy felt something stir inside. Without thinking she jumped in front of the little fox as another bullet whistled past. And another and another until finally the inevitable happened. She reeled as a bullet took a chunk out of the tower wall and ivory shrapnel shot through her body as though from a blunderbuss.

Granny moved closer with her gun poised, straining to see what was happening, what she had hit, for her eyesight was poor. The fox saw the hag lumbering towards them and stood on his hind legs, making himself as big as he could, so that he might take the bullet and, perhaps, save the girl. But the click click click of the gun proved the chamber to be empty and as granny huffed and puffed and stepped ever-closer, the beetle-thorn unfurled its tendrils and tightened them around her limbs and throat.

Poppy lay dead on the floor. Her blood was black in the full moon-light and her skin white like pearl. The last remnants of her unknown self, her fake lashes, peeled themselves from her lids and scuttled away, but didn't get far before losing the strength to carry on. They curled up and died beside her.

The fox hadn't even told her his name. He was full of a power he had never felt before. An aggression. A revulsion at a life taken too soon. As granny thrashed around in the shrub he bent to Poppy and began to lick her wounds. The blood beaded his whiskers and stained his teeth, his permanent grin and sodden tongue. It tasted good. Not like chicken. It tasted like wo-man. He began to paw at her dress, tearing at it to get to every bit of parted flesh, until it was shredded and she lay naked before him. He kept on licking at the blood that trickled persistently southbound as though she were lying on a slope, or the moon's gravitational pull held sway once more over all fluid motion. As he licked her skin he almost felt like he knew this woman, this gypsy witch who had lured him here only to save his life. This broken, bruised and nearly-scalped girl with deep blue eyes that looked now beyond him into remote other-worlds.

The fox began to sob, the tears spilling over and running down his snout, mixing with her blood on the end of his nose and falling in fat pink drops. It fell into her eyes, into her mouth which had slightly opened for her final exhalation, down her neck, between her breasts and suddenly she blinked. She drew in a breath. And then her whole body lunged forward in a kind of *danse macabre* and she writhed and fought madly as though possessed. And with one final spasm, the ivory splinters lodged in her body began to undo what can't be undone. They began to withdraw, to spiral up through the red of her heart until they popped out and lay like bloody dead bugs on the floor beside her. In their wake the lacerations began to shrink as the flesh slowly mended itself before the fox's eyes and Poppy opened her pretty blues and smiled at him. He looked around, dazed. Granny was still fighting the beetle-thorn but was losing the battle. Blood pooled from her withered, scratched skin and her movements were slow and tense; her screech had dwindled to a low-pitched wail.

The girl flung her arms around the fox's warm little body, his fur melting into her soft flesh. For one second, she wondered what she was do-ing, holding a fox so tight, a fox who smelled of blood, the fox perhaps that had been stealing granny's chickens. And then she remembered something. She wasn't sure what. It was a memory hidden behind layers of extraneous matter, pushed to the back of her mind where the grey whorls swirled like a fog over the Styx. She remembered, or felt she remembered, that she loved this fox. Pulling his head down close to hers and closing her eyes, she brought her pink lips to his black mouth. His meaty breath almost made her pull away, but then she felt his figure begin to transform in her arms. As fur gave way to smooth skin and limbs stretched to breaking point, his lips came into synch with hers and his tongue to playfully touch her own.

She opened her eyes.

"Felix?"

A man lay before her, naked, soft and hard, with yellow-brown eyes.

"Poppy? Of course."

"Felix. What the fuck? I mean, you were a fox?" Her heart pounded like it might explode, the scar tissue stretched taut like a drum.

"I don't know what happened, Poppy. I don't remember. But I love you. I love you so much. You took a bullet for me." He was looking at her body as he spoke and only then did she realise her nakedness. But she didn't feel embarrassed or vulnerable. She felt wonderfully exposed, shed of her superficiality, her kinks and defects. The black magic that had enveloped her had gone, the silver moon-magic of sex and passion and lunacy had returned and Poppy felt ready to embrace it, as the tides began to swell and the night-flowers gave off their sticky ripe scent so readily.

As she ran her hands over her body she became aware of red welts and muddy paw prints across her stomach and thighs. Felix looked down, ashamed. Poppy giggled. She knew all too well the magic of desire, the strength of lust. A potent mix indeed. The once-fox Felix now ran his long fingers over Poppy's body, happy to be rid of the soft pads and tearing claws. He wouldn't scratch her skin now. He would be gentle, feeling the depths and shallows with the very tips of his fingers. He would run his hands along the silken skin of her thighs, the skin no longer bruised and bleeding, healed at the same time the ivory liberated itself from her bloody chambers.

"I've wanted to touch you since the first time I saw you," he whispered. "Maybe that's why I was cursed to become a fox, because of my indecent thoughts."

Poppy laughed. "You're so silly. I've been thinking of you these last six months. Since you disappeared and took the moon with you. Every night I've wondered what you taste like, what you would feel like inside me. I've wanted to fuck you . . . until this no-moon became too much and I lost the will to . . . "

"You were thinking of me? And the whole time I was creeping around outside your tower, longing for you but not understanding why. The spell obviously eroded my memory, but retained my carnal desires."

"You animal!" she hissed, and kissed his cheeks, his forehead, his lips. She kissed his neck and inhaled the scent of him.

"I want your fingers inside me," she whispered into his chest. "I want to taste myself on you."

She moved down the length of his body to his erect penis and took him into her mouth, but he pushed her gently off him and laid her down on the floor. He knelt over her body, looking at her breasts, her indented waist and her hips like parentheses around her pubis. And then he began to lick the salt off her skin, the blood that had dried, the months of sadness, the lonely days and sleepless nights. He brought her feet up onto his shoulders and began to lick between her legs. Poppy felt everything drain out of her; she was melting into the grass. As he pushed one finger, and then another, inside her he circled her clitoris with his tongue and she whispered to herself "Felix, Felix, Felix".

All around them the sound of forest-rustling began, as small night animals appeared to watch and a little dog laughed to see such fun. Felix moved up the length of her body and kissed her.

"Can you taste yourself?"

She nodded.

"Don't you taste fucking unbelievable!"

She nodded again, almost lost in a fairytale world.

He eased his cock inside her. A perfect fit. As he began to move in a slow rhythm Poppy arched her back and moved in synch. When she raised her arms, that she might feel the penetration right through to the tips of her fingers and toes, he licked the sweat from her armpit. As they fucked he traced the outline of her lips with his fingers until she sucked them in and gently nibbled them.

And then the ground began to rumble. The soil loosened. The animals ran to their burrows and flew to their nests. The lovers barely noticed as their love-making grew faster and more furious. They wrestled and heaved and gasped and came and as they did, bunches of digitalis pushed themselves up through the soil, and stood there like soldiers. They formed a wall between the lovers and the tower. Foxglove, poisonous to some, deadly to others, and a sweet protection to those in need.

"What the hell is going on?" The voice of Poppy's father resounded through the night, stiff-upper-lipped and plumby. "Mother?" he shouted. "Mother! The bloody moon. Look at it. Where are you, old girl?"

As he stormed into the clearing, walking right past granny who was unconscious in her entanglement, Poppy and Felix jumped up and stood naked behind the wall of flowers.

"Poppy, put some bloody clothes on. And get away from that boy, NOW! He's vermin. He's dirty. He should be killed. He really should be dead; I don't understand it."

"What do you mean father?"

"I mean I cursed him. We, your granny and I, didn't want him sniffing around you so I did a little magic and turned him foxward. We knew under the spell that he wouldn't remember you. Unfortunately the moon took it upon herself to take umbrage."

Poppy flinched. "But you know granny shoots foxes for fun."

"Yes," he said, and that was all.

Poppy frowned. "Fuck you," she said.

"How dare you!" He shouted. His face was beginning to turn red and the veins in his neck to bulge.

"I demand that you return to your room this instant. If your mother were alive . . . "

"Yes, well, we all know why she isn't, don't we father?"

He answered her comment with silence and a scowl.

Felix whispered in her ear. "Come with me, girl. You can stay at mine. It's no ivory tower but I have a stove and hot water and a very comfortable bed on the floor. We can take it as slow as you like."

"Fuck that," she said. "I want to take it fast!"

And with that they joined hands and skipped into the forest, leaving her father lost for words and prevented from following by the foxglove that he dared not trample.

At Felix's small but comfortable home Poppy realised she had no clothes, no belongings, not a single thing with her.

"Oh, but that's alright," Felix said. "We don't need those things. We can live wild like animals, become true forest dwellers and enjoy the freedom the shade of the trees can offer."

Poppy smiled wryly and shimmied over to his bed: a single mattress on the floor. She knelt on all fours and patted her rump.

"Okay, but can we start by doing it doggy style?"

Felix bared his teeth and prepared to mount.

The Mythical Christine

by Jacqueline Houghton

The first time I heard her name? Yes, of course, I remember. I must have been about seven and I remember I was very proud of myself. I had managed to reverse the channels on the house system and instead of my parents listening to me, I could listen to them. I had achieved this great computing coup the previous night and had lain listening to them watching the wall. I had gone to sleep very quickly. Tonight again they were watching the wall, but this time something had caused a debate that rapidly led to shouting and drew my avid attention. I do not recall the exact details of the argument—it is, after all, nearly sixty years ago—but my mother accused my father of being sentimental and sensational, and my father accused my mother of falling for the propaganda. I had to run all three words through my Diannou and still did not fully understand what was said, but it was the first time I heard the name that has come to dominate my life—Christine Ying Xiong.

The first time I actually saw her I was twelve. I was at school and we were studying the Great Emigration. I am fourth generation, just far enough removed from those who knew the Earth as their home and remember the journey here. For you and me these worlds we live on are not new; they are not romantic, as they were portrayed in this particular history lesson. It is Earth now that is a mysterious, magic place lost to all. A source of much speculation and ever-growing myths and legends. I am particularly fond of the Earth as Heaven idea. I rather like the idea of our souls returning to their original planet. It has a certain charm and a certain irony, given so many people were persuaded to make the journey to the New Worlds as a kind of rapture—a flight to Heaven.

Anyway, back to my school lesson. All four walls are active and our group is surrounded by images of the time. Even now, despite a life time of these experiences, I find it disconcerting to be at once in the middle of the mob and yet unable to touch, to interact, to influence what is going on around me. And we are in the middle of a vast crowd watching a select few on a platform, their images magnified on walls behind them. There are long speeches on the glory of the moment—I am twelve and I am bored. My interest inflates at the sight of the behemoth hanging in space; the camera beams us inside and we are surrounded by the happy, waving crew. Ten thousand souls are on board and already asleep for this epic journey. They and those to follow over the next few years are the ones who will scratch a civilization from the dirt of the New Worlds. A new infestation is setting out across the universe—my words, not those of the speech makers. The film pans back to the crowds and to the speeches. I am distracted by Jessalyn. She is standing very close to me and I can smell her skin warming in the heat of the classroom. And then a name blows away the scent of blossoming hormones—Christine Ying Xiong. I look up and there on the wall is the image of a woman. She is that pleasing mix of Asian and Caucasian—dark eyes, fine bones and straight hair. Yet there is a hardness in the set of her face, in her actions as she pounds the podium with the palm of her hand. She rails against the lazy platitudes of the earlier speakers. They watch her uneasily.

'We are the billions,' she roars. 'You.' She points at her fellow speakers. 'You with your pampered lives and billowing dreams, forget that each and every one of us has a soul that cannot be ignored.'

'Light.' The images on the walls fade and the room is illuminated once again.

'No, don't stop.' Caught up in the moment I speak without thinking and am rewarded with laughter those around me.

'We will carry on tomorrow,' the teacher says.

But we do not carry on the next day; the story jumps to the New Worlds, leaving Earth and Christina behind. And my youthful self is distracted once more by Jessalyn Chenkova.

Now then, look here, I am rather proud of this. I drew it myself from memory of that first meeting with Christina. I think I've captured her likeness rather well, don't you? Don't touch the screen, it's very old.

Why was I so drawn to Christine Ying Xiong—Chrissie, Christa, Krystina? Her name changes over the years with the different memories I have consulted. I have been asked that question many times. The answer is simple, as I realised very early on, but let me carry on with my story first.

I am sixteen; I have long moved on from Jessalyn and am being distracted by Ian Barbari. We did the projects then, of course, not like now, and it was thanks to Ian that I focused on the role of politicians during the Great Emigration for my project—and of course, Christine Ying Xiong. Even then my choice of topic was queried. I chose my subject matter after a careless comment by Ian about how we were being made to worship the past and those who had brought us here to the New Worlds. He was not referring to Christina as such (despite the impression I may have given you so far, her role in events was very different). I retorted that his ancestors could have stayed on Earth to shrivel in the heat with their crops, or drown in the floods with their animals, but had shown better sense for which he should be grateful. We spent the evening fighting over the merits of the Great Emigration and how different our lives might have been. The next morning I chose my project just so I could prove him wrong.

I was only partially successful in this. Events were not as simple as I had previously believed and it is from here that my understanding of how a story, which everyone knows to be true, can vary so widely in its details between each teller and each tale that the definition of the word truth has to be questioned.

Let me give you an example. One drawn directly from my project. I stumbled across this recording in an old archive, being very proud of myself for finding it. It took a lot of patience. Listen.

"Christie knew. She saw the perma droughts, the drownins. She saw the pinchi. The president thems glory all, glory all. Not happy at Christie. She was in the high camps. She shouted truth. Presidents covered ears. She's dead. Not gone on. Not gone on to space. Presidents they lie. They do her. Orai? We follow . . . "

It breaks up there completely. I've run every program I know to restore it over the years but it's beyond recovery. As a clip it is rather unrepresentative of much I have to show you. But it is that urgent voice. The voice of a young person possibly not much older than I was at the time. Finding this as a sixteen year old, I smelled conspiracy, I smelled discovery, I smelled excitement. It propelled me onwards. What else was hidden in this vast store of information? It was then

I discovered my love of the hunt, the chase. The vast metabases were my world. I stalked through their mazes. My weapons were my intellect and my curiosity, words were my keys—find the right one, the right combination and bases unlock. Now listen to this one, again only the voice is preserved. Very different.

"I knew Chris as well as anyone. She was driven and passionate and unpleasant if you didn't agree with her. She had a way with those in the high camps. ____ cunning; she stopped them seeing her wealth and power and what she was really doing. ____ safe beacon who drew all dissenters ____ she ranted, they listened. In allowing her to protest and rage, she proved nothing ____. After all, if it was ____ would not have let her continue."

You see what I mean? A different, and much more critical view, but did you notice the drop-outs? I do believe it has been tampered with—fascinating in itself.

My project received rather average marks. I did well for effort and research, they said, but they questioned my somewhat 'adolescent' conclusions. With the benefit of an adult's eye I can see I may have overstated certain aspects and that my shouts of conspiracy may have been overly shrill. However, my project realised in me a desire for knowledge and truth, and released my inquisitive nature into the metabases.

I studied history and politics and have followed an academic career since —with a few excursions into the media world. I have continued my interest in Christine and have slowly created this archive of material. I have also developed some interesting, and some might say provocative, theories on the events surrounding the Emigration which is, of course, why you are here. But I jump ahead.

It is interesting, the nature of information about the Emigration. Much was lost in the chaos of the times and it has not been a straightforward matter for anyone interested in the subject to get a clear, untainted view of what happened. Part of the excitement of the subject, I think. Most historians have focussed on the great leaders, the last on Earth and the first ones on the New Worlds, and I can see why. Humanity, certainly the first generation or so, wanted to know it had made the correct decision in coming here—that it had acted in the best interests of everyone. Even now there are many people who do not want to hear what I have to say and feel threatened when I speak. Only the other day, I was conversing with a friend who suggested I should tone down some of the language I use in my new book, but as I explained to him, he had (and he is not alone in this) failed to grasp the difference between opinion and fact. A subtle point for some, but I do my best to make it clear. I digress. We were talking about the nature of the information. Most is from the metabases. I sometimes feel I have spent more of my life immersed in them than I have in the real world. It is a skilled process following ancient and intricate leads through the bases but ultimately a rewarding one. I have been fortunate that my career has allowed me into areas not accessible to everyone, and that I have been able to use and indeed have helped develop some of the most sophisticated of recovery programs.

But there are other, rarer sources. Knowing of my interest in the subject, people have come forward with personal data either lost from or never stored on the bases. These are often fascinating in that they are unique. I am, however, always cautious—there are many vested interests in the subject these days.

For example, consider this. It is a recording from a personal base— always something to be suspicious of.

"Met Christine Ying Xiong. Discussed the matter. Garrett and Perez are pinchi. Bena transport. Malakova—fund. Ghorashi and Izundi ready. Han—Moscow. Abdullah—Berlin. Fei—Beijing. Wait till Congress signs, then go fast."

Too convenient, don't you think? General Garrett and Edan Perez were, as you know, assassinated. Strange that such an inflammatory snippet should be "discovered" so long after the event. Strange too that it should so neatly mention several Ziru leaders, yet appear to be from before that organization existed. I think this is a deliberate and rather unsophisticated attempt to tarnish her reputation and mine. So you see, one must always be sceptical.

The rarest of all information is hard copies. These are often duplicates of what already appear on the bases but, just occasionally, an original is discovered. These are always the subject of huge debate and often of controversy—provenance is all. Are you familiar with the Tiksi Portfolio? No? Let me show you a copy. Not the original of course. That is preserved in a secure environment; I am not allowed to say where. Give me a moment and I will find it for you.

Here we are. It's on the bases now but there is something rather inspiring about seeing it in its original hard copy form. Notice the date: 2108. Just before the exodus.

"The South European States (SES) has been accused of concealing a water extraction plant in defiance of international calls for transparency over its plans. The leaders of the Northern European States (NES) and the Sino-Russia Republics (SRR) have demanded immediate access to the facility to establish the source, quantity and quality of the water involved. The SES only acknowledged the existence of the plant on Wednesday saying it was not yet operational and would only be used in the event of imminent collapse of the State's water supplies.

"The SES's decision to build a secret facility represents a fundamental challenge to international collaboration over the disputed water supplies of the continent," Krystyna Geroj of the Sino-Russian Republics said. "They must comply with their obligations under the Fair Distribution and Conservation of Water Treaty signed last year."'

A different person? No I don't think so. Hers is an interesting name—-Christine, from the Greek translation of the Hebrew word for Messiah, has many spellings and Geroj is the Russian translation of Ying Xiong, both of which roughly mean "hero" in English.

Krystyna Geroj was a frequent spokesperson for the SRR. Here's another example from the portfolio.

"A SES court has sentenced sixty people to death over ethnic unrest in the Lombardy 2 High Camp in September, state-run media report. Nearly 1000 people were killed during riots between African, European and Arab ethnic groups. A further 225 people who have been tried this week on charges including murder, robbery and arson. A protest at the lack of sanitation in the camp on 5 July quickly erupted into violence, leaving at least 1000 dead and another 4,200 injured. Entire blocks were smashed and set alight and passers-by and would be rescuers attacked by rioters. Disturbances continued for nearly a week as the army struggled to restore order. Thousands of people were detained after the violence and 285 people have now been convicted with another 490 awaiting trial. Tensions between the different groups in the high camps have been growing as tens of thousands of new immigrants have been moved into the region in the past few months. Commenting on the sentences, Krystyna Geroj of the SRR said the SES has exaggerated the threat to justify harsh controls. 'These trials are a sham. They have lacked transparency and fairness and the sentences are likely to further inflame tensions in the area."'

The portfolio as you may have gathered is a series of these short articles. Not all mention Krystyna, but many do. They give a flavour, a bitter flavour, of the times.

Now then, let me get you that drink and we can look at our subject properly from the beginning.

There you are. Now then, Christina was born in the north of the SRR possibly on the island of Novaya Zemlya sometime around 2069. There is no surviving documentation of her birth. I have garnered the information from comments made by both herself and others. She appears to have had two older brothers, both of whom were in the army and one of whom was killed (although how is unclear). Her eldest brother emigrated, that is certain. He never had children and Christina has no direct descendants—at least, not here on the New Worlds. I will explain in due course. Her childhood experiences are unknown. Given she grew up on the great Arctic seaway, I imagine it would have been cosmopolitan and to some extent protected from the worst of the chaos further south. No, I don't believe she ever married. Certainly I have found no records of a partner. She worked, at least initially, for the government of the SSR, as we can see from the Tiksi portfolio. However, at some point, she must have left this post as her later stance is clearly not that of any of the major governments. However, her initial role as spokesperson for the government gave her access to the full horrors of the times in which she found herself living. Whilst in the two reports I have shown you she is clearly outraged at the behaviour of others, one feels she is merely reflecting her government's position. This next report is different. It is well preserved—full pictures (only flat screen of course), not just sound this time and I think you will agree that, although it is a report she sent back to the government, this is not someone following a line they have been given. It is the Tianjin drowning. She spent a lot of time in the area after the floods, talking to and helping the survivors. It's one of the most complete pieces of her journalism we have. I'll play it in full.

"Seven million people. Seven million people. Why did seven million people have to die here? Does that number mean anything to anyone any more? I am angry, so angry. The levees failed. Why did the levees fail? Why did the defences not stand? There have been floods before. There have been cyclones. We have always defended the land from the sea and from the rivers. Why not this time? Does no one see what is happening?

"A month ago, this place was 100km from the coast. Now the sea stretches before me. It has redrawn its boundaries. It has taken three cities, countless small settlements and seven million souls. It has worked with the rivers to create a vast new landscape of hills built from broken debris, meanders of stinking, chemical sludge and endless expanses of mud. Everywhere there is mud. It ponds around my feet as I walk. It traps vehicles, fills buildings that still stand and invades the hastily erected emergency shelters. It smothers the bodies of the dead and the living. It is as though it is trying to cover up what has happened, to bury all evidence that there was once anything else here. Rain is forecast again. The rivers are back to normal levels but they now follow new routes snaking across this changed landscape.

"Looking out across the sea, I can see the remains of buildings still jutting above the shallow waters, standing like memorials. Pan the camera, there. They are the only memorials most of the dead will know. Entire communities, entire generations dead. Dead but not gone. Bodies and body parts, both human and animal float in with each tide, carried gently by the sea and laid on the mud by the waves. It is as though the sea knows they do not belong to her and she is returning them home. People come and search after every high tide looking for their lost loved ones.

"The land is saturated. Attempts to dig mass graves have done nothing more than create new lakes. So instead, diggers work amongst the searchers piling the remains of the swollen and decomposing bodies on to transporters for burial further inland. The stink of decay saturates the air and, as I walk, I am forced to step over dismembered, rotting, fly infested arms, legs, hands and heads. There are no words for this. These were once people.

"There are still people here. Not just those searching for the lost. There are people who lived here, unable to leave, who sit staring at the sea, waiting for it to retreat and give them back their homes. They do not seem to hear those who tell them their land is gone forever. Others, ever hopeful, search amongst the living for familiar faces. There are doctors, nurses, soldiers, journalists and politicians. There is some semblance of organisation. It is, after all, four weeks since the breach and three weeks since the waters settled, at least for now. Tents stretch to the horizon. There are hospital tents, disease control now more than to treat injuries from the flood. Typhoid and cholera are already a problem; drinking water is being trucked in but there is never enough. Information tents where vague efforts are made to list the living and the dead. Tents for those to wait in for transport to take them elsewhere. Tents for those who sit and stare.

"I have talked to many of the survivors. There are tales of bravery, luck and desperate sadness, but through the shock the tales are the same. There was no warning and nowhere to go when the defences failed, and this brings me back to my original question. Why did the defences fail? They have stood sound through worse storms. Why did they fail so dramatically? I know the rivers were swollen from the monsoon; I know the cyclone was vast, the wind ferocious and the sea surge high, but this land is precious. Food—vast areas of wheat, rice and maize grew here vital to our country's security. How could we have allowed this land to be lost? And why now? Why when we already face shortages from the droughts? We knew this storm was coming. Surely the defences were checked and rechecked before it struck? We will all grow hungry because they failed."

Very moving, don't you think? Very moving. Sometimes I think how lucky we are to be safe on these New Worlds, but then again, I look around me and wonder what, if anything, has really changed.

I believe Christina's intense interest in the Tianjin drowning may have been due to part of her family coming from this area of eastern China. It is quite possible that she had relatives who died there, although she does not mention them. Her passion, her fire, is quite unlike anything seen in her earlier reports. I think this marks a vital change for Christine; a vital change in her life's purpose. And the clue is in her repeated question—why did the defences fail?

Of course, after such a tragedy there are many investigations. Engineers, scientists, journalists, politicians, all inspected, examined, scrutinised and probed this question. I suppose you could say there were the usual set of answers: the unfortunate coincidence of high river levels due to unusually heavy monsoon rains; the unpredictable track of the cyclone which meant the barriers were raised a few hours later than was ideal; an unexpected technical failure on one of the barrier's sealing mechanisms; the unforeseen consequences of this minor failure on the unconsolidated river sediments beneath it; the unrelated collapse of several short sections of coastal flood banks and river levees all many kilometres apart; and the unanticipated way these events coalesced into a disaster of such unimaginable proportions. Everyone blamed someone else. A few minor technicians were hanged and those unaffected by the drowning moved on.

But not Christine. Something was wrong and she knew it. Her story becomes harder to follow for a while. There are no further reports from her for the SRR government that I have found. She is mentioned by other people and can be seen at reports on the Bremen and Shanghai drownings, but nothing from her directly, until I found this. It is a news conference held shortly after the York drowning. I've edited it slightly so we come straight in as Christina starts to ask questions.

"Why so many floods?"

"I cannot answer for other places but we were managing the retreat of this area."

"65,000 dead is not managing a situation. Who is responsible for this?"

"Nobody is responsible; it was an act of god or mother nature. There is only so much we can do."

"It is the same company that built the defences here that built them in Bremen, Tianjin and Shanghai. Why were the barriers not checked again after the floods in Germany and China?"

"They were checked. They are checked and maintained on a regular basis. There was nothing wrong with them."

"But clearly there was. They failed. 65,000 people are dead and many more injured and homeless. There is a fault in the design. In the sealing mechanism along the inner barriers. It has been found in every enquiry after a major flood."

"I've never heard of such a fault."

"But surely you've read the SES government's report on Bremen, version

1.3?"

"I have read all the reports. There is no such fault. You are wasting my time."

"You cannot have read them all. There are some the company's kept hidden. Ask Trebula for Bremen 1.3. See what they say."

Christine was arrested just after this encounter, allegedly for breach of the peace. She was released again almost immediately.

There has been a great deal of research and speculation over the years as to why so many places had to flood catastrophically with such vast loss of life. The consensus is that in a world beset by food shortages and lack of space, low-lying land was too valuable either for agriculture or for living space to be abandoned and was defended far beyond what was technologically possible thus ensuring disaster was only a matter of time. I am normally of the opinion that the simplest answer is the best, but in this case I think not. I have tracked down one of the reports that Christina refers to and it does indeed refer to a manufacturing problem with some of the components of the sealing units. However, it claims it had no impact on the overall effectiveness of the units and was in no way responsible for the failure of these particular barriers. On its own still the simplest answer stands, but it is not on its own. In following Christine through the metabases I have found many examples of accidents and disasters either caused by or made worse by technical failures or unaccountable actions by those in authority. For example, here Christine and a representative from Sanwan Industries being interviewed by a news channel on the failure of the Gothenburg desalinisation plant. Again, I have edited it to start with Christine.

"This plant supplied water to several million people. It supplied water to the Island High Camp. There are over a million people there alone and conditions are deteriorating rapidly. Diseases are already beginning to spread as the sanitation system breaks down. Yet there seems no hurry to repair the damage."

"We are working as fast as possible to solve the problem. We are aware of the consequences of this breakdown and are shipping in drinking water from around the North European States, but the government is blocking us from using many supplies. They say we must work within the rations."

"How could you allow such a vital plant to fail? Surely you have mechanisms in place to ensure this could not happen?"

"I cannot comment in detail as we do not have the full technical report yet, but it would seem a minor error triggered an unexpected chain reaction of breakdowns. We have many components that need replacing or repairing and then testing before the plant can become safely operational again."

"How long will that be?"

"I cannot say at the moment."

"There have been several charges of sabotage, most notably by one of your own directors. What do you have to say on this?"

"The possibility of terrorism has not been ruled out but who would stand to gain from such actions?"

"The discontent, the deteriorating conditions in the High Camp, all push people towards emigration. Your company, Sanwan Industries, is a major supplier of equipment to the New Worlds Consortium. I would have thought you stood to gain a great deal from the failure of your plants here on Earth."

"Ziru sees conspiracy theories everywhere, Christina. I will not dignify them with a reply. Sanwan Industries is dedicated to supplying safe, clean drinking water to people round the world. We operate under increasingly difficult circumstances. We work hard to maintain the quality and reliability of the water supplies. Unfortunately, occasionally there are failures, as in any other industry, but we work hard to ensure repairs are carried out quickly and supplies restored."

As you can tell, Christina takes charge of the interview. This is the earliest reliable reference to Ziru I have discovered. Christine is one of its founding members. It was a coming together of groups that opposed the governments, the emigration to the New Worlds, the big corporations, the disaffected in general. You've never heard of them? No, I'm not surprised. Ziru was very active for a period of some ten years before the governments grew tired of it and its members were arrested, executed, suffered forced emigration or just disappeared. But I am jumping ahead of myself. Here is an example of Christine in action with Ziru in its early days, as reported by the major news channel of the time.

"This is Xavier Al-Hakeem reporting for SSR News Inc. Today it was Moscow's turn to see the full fury of a Ziru protest and Red Square yet again was the centre of the action. The protest was initially peaceful and the thousands gathered listened to speeches by the Ziru leader Christina Ying Xiong."

"We need to focus on what is important. On why we are here. The Emigration is flawed. It will not save us. It serves no purpose but to make the corporations ever richer. So many of us are frustrated by it. We want change here on Earth not some far away planets. That is why we are here today. We do not want violence. Just for our voices to be heard. It is unbelievable to me how we are being manipulated and brainwashed into believing this is the best path for humanity. There is a huge swath of dissatisfied citizens out there who feel the same and here we can come together to make a voice bigger than any of our own. The propaganda machine is a sham to keep us confused and lose us in its complexities of pseudo-science and prophecies of disasters. There is no need for us to leave Earth. We can save the land and we can save the people."

What follows are a series of clips I have gathered from the news reports of the day.

"The crowds are chanting 'freedom, Ziru, peace'. There must be easily a hundred thousand people here. There is music and dancing. It's like a giant party; the atmosphere is festive. So far it is noisy but peaceful."

"Police are trying to clear the area in front of the Cathedral. They have re-opened the road there and are encouraging protesters to disperse along it. A few missiles are thrown and there is a lot of chanting. Some of crowd appear to be moving on."

"The crowd are attentive as their leaders speak. They clap, cheer or whistle as required."

"I admit Christina can be a bit extreme and I wouldn't say every word is the whole truth but she gets us heard. She is showing us who is really responsible for this nightmare we've gotten into."

"From this vantage point, I can see groups of soldiers putting on riot gear and van loads of police with dogs are arriving. The police have blocked off all approaches to the Red Square, they are letting a few people out but no one back in again."

"The crowd outside the Kremlin is getting increasingly tense. The demonstrators are beginning to surge forward pushing against the police lines."

"Why protest? We have the solution. Agreed it's flawed and rough but it's viable and it's our only chance. Those who don't agree should be allowed to stay here and rot."

"The demonstrators are not free to move around. The police are closing off street after street. Protesters are trapped in the square."

"It's just after three o'clock and the riot police are charging at the demonstrators. I don't know why, but I can see people being beaten and trampled underfoot."

"It was like we weren't there. Like we were part of the ground. They just walked over us. If you moved they beat you till you stopped."

"We can confirm that the number of people arrested now stands at 832. There are two confirmed deaths both from natural causes. 18 police and four soldiers have been hospitalized with injuries. We do not have exact figures for injured protesters but it is estimated to be around 215."

"I don't understand. We did nothing to provoke them. We just wanted to go home, but they wouldn't let us out of the Square."

"Only two dead? And of natural causes? Two hundred I say, if not more. Look for the photographs, the films. There are plenty of them. All the evidence is there."

The protests did seem to follow the same pattern in each city round the world—initially peaceful rallies, speeches, perhaps a few hecklers as would be expected, but then as the crowds began to disperse something would change. Whether it was elements within the crowd determined to cause trouble despite their leaders' pleas, whether it was police or soldiers panicking at the numbers of people involved or whether there really were darker motives on the part of the authorities it is difficult to say. Perhaps a combination of all three, but over time, these demonstrations tainted Ziru's image. A movement that started out peacefully protesting at what it saw as a disastrous choice by those in power to abandon the planet became seen as a terrorist organisation determined to destroy humanity's last chance of freedom.

There were many bombings, arson attacks, attacks within the metabases, murders, kidnappings and so on attributed to Ziru activists. Many of its members were tried and convicted. Some possibly were guilty. Any organisation the size of Ziru, with its anti-government stance, was bound to attract malcontents who commandeered its message and used it as an excuse to vent their anger against the state. Many, though, proclaimed their innocence right up until their executions. The Ziru leaders, Christina included, constantly denied any connection with these nefarious activities. They expressed great distress that Ziru's name and peaceful purposes were being polluted by the activities of a few and they accused other organisations including major corporations and the state itself of being behind many of the incidents.

However, the most infamous event was, of course, the Vostochny Spaceport bombing. The destruction of a space ship with all those on board—ten thousand souls, plus five hundred and thirty on the ground. It was a dreadful, dreadful act. The Sino-Soviet Republic blamed Ziru within an hour of the news of the bombing. Ziru through Christine responded thus:

"Those of us at Ziru would like to express our utmost horror and revulsion at this most barbaric of attacks. We would like to state in the strongest terms possible that no one at Ziru was responsible in any way for what happened at the Spaceport. We are a genuine and legal organisation totally committed to peaceful acts of protest. We in no way endorse, condone or encourage acts of violence. Ziru, and myself personally, would like to express our deepest condolences to all those affected by this terrible tragedy."

Denials were not enough. Twenty seven members of Ziru including three of its leaders were arrested, tried and found guilty of the bombing. It was too much for the organisation. It was branded a terrorist group and membership was made illegal. It collapsed under the weight of allegations and counter allegations from within and without. The remaining leaders were either arrested or went into hiding. Christine did the latter.

The rest of her story is almost entirely told by others now. There is some legal paper work which suggests she died two years later. However, it's authenticity was questioned even at the time. A more popular rumour was that she had finally discovered evidence of who was really behind the Spaceport bombing and was assassinated before she could reveal it. This has a certain appeal. I have discovered many documents in the bases that make various claims as to who the perpetrators were. Personally, I feel one should look for the party or the parties which stood to gain from such an atrocity. Certainly Ziru were anti-emigration.

Their raison d'être was for humanity to remain on Earth and deal with the envir-onmental situation, not run away to an unknown, uncertain and possibly unsafe future on another pair of planets. To some this may seem a motive enough to destroy a space ship; to physically prevent people from leaving. However, it resul-ted, at worst, in a minor delay whilst another ship was built—at the height of the emigration there were over two hundred ships making the return journey every four weeks and some of these ships were capable of carrying three hundred thousand people, thirty times that of the ship destroyed. If Ziru had really wanted to delay the Emigration why not attack one of the largest vessels not one of the smallest?

Remember, at the time, there was no guarantee the Emigration would be successful. There were other influential groups as well as Ziru arguing that either some or all of humanity should remain on Earth. It was not universally agreed that everyone should go. It is hard to believe that anyone associated with an anti-emigration group such as Ziru would not realise the consequences of killing so many people. Of course it would lead to a backlash. Of course it gave new vigour to the emigration campaigns. Of course it served to destroy not only Ziru but most of the other anti-emigration movements as well. So who had the most to gain from such a spectacular catastrophe? I think it is clear. It fits in with the pattern. The pattern that Christina was painting in every interview, in every broadcast. Those in power, those with money, the big corporations, they stood to gain from a mass emigration. How else could they continue to profit? Millions of "customers" were dying. The only way for humanity to successfully continue to live on Earth was to make radical changes. Changes that did not suit these big corporations. Look how it is here now. We have brought our old problems with us, carried here like fleas on a dog. You look scandalised but nothing has really changed.

I don't believe Christine was assassinated then or later. Despite all the setbacks, resistance to the Emigration continued. Efforts were more subdued; those involved had been driven underground, but there is plenty of evidence of their activities. Here's a virus that was scattered across the metabases. A popular form of communication amongst the movement; I have many examples like it.

"It is hot. It is dry. But it is not infertile. Why abandon the land?

Why don't we irrigate the fields when we have the technology?

Why don't we prevent the loss soil when we are the engineering capability?

Why don't we plant the crops that will grow in poor soils when we have the agricultural expertise?

Why is this land not productive when there are billions of mouths to feed?

"Save the land. Save the people."

"Save the land. Save the people." A phrase used often by Christina. It was her rallying cry and one heard again and again.

Here is an interesting account. It is an official report on the activities of those opposed to the state. As you can imagine it took a great deal of finding and even once I had found it, I kept it to myself until it seemed safe to reveal its existence. It is a long document so I have highlighted the relevant sections.

"There is no coherent leadership of this group. However, there are individuals whose presence seems to inspire others. Of interest particular interest is one Linlin Grebenkova, also known as Krys Uchimura. Her metabase identities are believed to include Surama, Har7rier and XYacoV3. She is 158cm tall, slight build, short grey hair, brown eyes and with pronounced scars across her upper back and arms. There are confirmed sightings of this person in Yakutsk on 7, 10 and 11 February and 18 and 19 April 2141 and an unconfirmed sighting on 24 May. As Surama she is responsible for the series of unsuccessful viral attacks on the metabases of the Vostochny Spaceport, the SSR government and the SSR army base at Amga."

They say unsuccessful, of course, but there was a three week break in departures in the spring of 2141 that has never been satisfactorily explained. And before you ask, I believe this is Christine because it fits with her modus operandi of non-violent protest, the Chinese/Russian name, her alternative pseudonym Krys, almost dangerously close to her real name and most importantly the choice of metabase identity—Surama. Surama is hero in Hindi. This is Christine. A woman of remarkable courage, determined not to be silent on a subject she believes to be of vital importance.

Have you ever considered why no-one was allowed to stay behind?

CABALA

Would it have mattered if a few, willing souls were left behind to make what they could of their lives? Why were such determined efforts made to ensure not one single human being remained on the planet? It seems a little extreme, don't you think? Not even a small group to monitor Earth—to keep the house warm, if you like. A base to which to return to if necessary. We were not a contamination on Earth. We were not some contagious disease every last remnant of which needed to be removed for recovery to take place. A few small communities scattered in the more habitable areas round the planet or even one larger base would have been possible. Oh I know the arguments. It was too political. Who would stay behind? Who would decided who stayed behind? The numbers would have needed to be exact from each state, but the larger states wanted more representatives. And what was to prevent a quick genocide of any one group after everyone else had left? It was too dangerous, too political and too expensive. After all, some sort of contact would need to be maintained. Those who remained behind would not expect to be abandoned. No, no, it was much simpler for everyone to leave. Every last person on Earth would make the journey to the New Worlds whether they wanted to or not. Yet how can democracies achieve such a feat? It is hardly a democratic act. Of course it was dressed up as salvation and a chance to start again. I do not deny that the vast number of people came here willingly, even eagerly. With the rising sea levels, the droughts, the floods, the storms, the famines, the wars, there was not much to stay for. But a democracy cannot force people to act against their nature. There were no democracies left at the end of the Emigration and we have brought that same authoritarian corporatocracy with us to the New Worlds.

What do I say to those who claim I am deluded and obsessed? That I am a fantasist? I say look around you. Look on the metabases, in our cities and towns. All is not well. These ideas are not mine, they are not new. They have been around ever since the time of the Emigration. It is just sometimes they have been voiced louder than others. And now is the time to shout them out loud. We need to understand why we moved here and what the full consequences of this have been. People have new diseases, cancers and viruses that have never been seen before. More and more young people are infertile. I know the arguments: the better medical care we have, the longer people live, the more likely we are to see new illnesses; yes, it's still a new planet and there are bugs still being discovered, that infertility is a minor inconvenience, easily treatable. But does that not concern you? What will we do if it is this world making us sick? Look for yet more planets to inhabit? There are those who say when we came here we came to Heaven. If that is true then we invaded Heaven too early. It was not ready for us. It is not happy with us. However, it is more important now to concentrate on what we should do and this is where I think all that I have said about Christine is key. She has a message that is as relevant today as it was at the time of the Emigration. We should have stayed on Earth and addressed the problems we created. Things are not as perfect here as promised. Humanity was born on Earth. It was born to be on Earth and we should go back.

What was that? You're changing the subject again? Do my ideas make you that uncomfortable or do you just disagree with them? Oh, the question earlier. I do apologize. I have often asked it of myself over the years and it is not difficult to answer. It is her passion for the planet of her birth. It is a passion I have come to share as I have traced and tracked, explored and examined, scrutinized and analysed her story through the metabases. I have met her many times; she permeates the bases like a transforming virus. I feel she has come to walk beside me. She has taken my hand and shown me her story. She has done this for a reason and it is imperative as a society we take notice of her again. But I will talk more on this shortly. I have one more important piece to show you. I have further evidence that Christine survived right to the end of the Emigration, right up until the last of the metabases on Earth were dismantled and any remaining proof of her existence would be impossible to maintain.

And here it is, my most momentous find. Solid evidence that Christine was alive and on Earth right at the end of the Emigration. I have held back its release. I wanted to be absolutely certain that it is indeed genuine and has not been tampered with in any way.

It is the transcript of the interrogation of a young woman. The beginning of the interview is so badly corrupted I will not play it here. But from it I have been able to retrieve her name, which is Helenka Koh, and the fact that she was arrested during a raid on an illegal camp hidden deep in the new Russian wilderness.

Notice she appears both injured and drugged. They were not gentle with her.

"How many of you are there?"

"Thirty, forty."

"How long have you been there?"

"I said how long?

"Orai, orai. Months, I think."

"And the others? How long has the camp existed?"

"Two, three years."

"I want names."

"No names. Never used names."

"You must have called each other something. Nicknames? Pseudonyms? Codenames? Everyone has some sort of name."

"No names."

"Orai, let's try something else. How did you find the camp? It is too well hidden to stumble upon by chance. Who took you there?"

"A man."

"What was his name?"

"Don't know."

"How did you meet him?"

"In a bar."

"How original. Where?"

"Moscow."

"Where exactly?"

"Don't remember. Near Red Square, one of the back streets."

"How did you meet? Did you arrange it or did he?"

"I followed Surama through the bases. She took me there."

"She took you to the bar?"

"No, no. She showed me the way through the bases. I traced the viruses, that's how I found him, how I knew him."

"What did he look like?"

"Tall as you, thinner. Kept his face hidden."

"What did you do in this bar?"

"Talked about the war.

"Did you tell him you wanted to stay behind?"

"Enough I was there. You don't say it aloud."

"What happened then?"

"We drove, somewhere on the edge of the city, dunno where exactly. Stayed there a few days. Then drove, walked, rode horses even. Always at night, dunno where I was."

"But you wanted to be there."

"Yes."

"Who was in charge at this camp? There must have been some sort of leadership."

"No-one in charge, just altogether."

"I don't believe you. Who was there first? Who chose this hiding place? Somebody must have been making decisions. Who were they? What was their name?"

"No, no."

"Orai, I need a piss. We will carry on later."

There is an edit here, before it continues again.

"Orai, I want names. Names will get you out of here. Names will get you a drink and something to eat. Names will get those wounds treated. Names will get you a bed and some rest. Names will get you a nice berth on a ship and a new life at the other end."

"Don't want . . . new life."

"You won't have this one much longer if you don't give me names. I want the names of the leaders in the camp and I want as many names as you can remember. I'll up the dose again if I have to."

"No! . . . no real . . . names . . . names we called each other."

"That will do."

"Yang, Matt . . . Dmytro . . . Yuri, Ang . . . Please no . . . "

"Keep going."

"Ah! Suelee . . . Bear . . . Alex, Olha . . . Nadine . . . "

"You said there were thirty to forty of you. You must know more."

"Sash . . . Oki. Stop, please."

"And which of these was in charge? Which one of these was your leader?"

"No . . . she . . . no . . . "

"Come on, stay with us."

"No, ah . . . Linlin . . . Surama . . . "

"Helenka, Helenka. Wake up, Helenka. Ah, fuck. Someone get a medic."

Helenka Koh's death is recorded as 10/05/2131. That is right at the end of the Emigration period. Whether it was as a direct result of these events or later, I don't know, but she did at least get her wish to remain on Earth.

I'm sorry, you look disturbed. It is not easy viewing, I agree. Here, take a moment. I hope, though, you see my point in showing you it.

Christine did not emigrate, of this I am certain. A political activist of such voracity would not have gone meekly into a spacecraft. She would have resisted. I don't believe she was forcibly emigrated under another name either. There is no evidence for anyone with her pseudonyms arriving in the New Worlds and every last person was documented on departure from Earth and again on arrival. I also doubt the capture of such an important figure by the state would have gone unrecorded. If she had been arrested, there would be evidence. So Christine Ying Xiong/Krystyna Geroj/Surama fought the Emigration and its consequences right to the end.

What? Is it not obvious? Have I not just said? She remained behind. I believe the evidence of this young woman tortured by the authorities into giving up her name. Christina escaped capture and stayed on Earth.

Oh I can see you look incredulous. There was nobody left behind. I know that. We all know that. We were brought up believing every last soul came to the New Worlds. Left the Earth free to recover from its experiment in sentience. Free to return to its pre-human state. Free to return to the Garden of Eden. Not one person could be left behind. How could they? The planet was swept for signs of intelligent life for nearly ten years before the last soldiers left the space station and came to the New Worlds. How could anybody have hoped to have stayed behind?

But planets are huge and the Earth has many places that could have hidden a determined community. Don't look so worried. It's not treason to speculate. I often wonder what it was like. It must have been a strange existence. Did they know they were being watched from space? Quite possibly. Did they ever feel safe to wander through deserted cities as nature claimed back what was hers or did they spend what was left of their lives hiding in caves, like nocturnal creatures, only venturing out under cover of darkness? Did any of them change their minds and try to contact what they hoped were watchers in the sky? I don't know. I have found no evidence of the last crew of the space station reporting anything other than boredom.

I think there is every possibility at least one, if not more, communities still exist on Earth. Like guardian spirits, taking care of the birthplace of humanity. When we return, as I believe we must, we will find Christina's descendants waiting for us.

I know there are people who disagree, often in the strongest of terms, with what I have to say. Some argue my ideas are dangerous, that I am a radical stirring up discontent. Your unease during this interview suggests you believe this. Did you know I have been followed? That I have received death threats? Some try to castrate my arguments by saying that in allowing me to speak un-censored the authorities prove me wrong. These same disparaging remarks were made about Christina and I am proud of the comparison. I carry her voice, her ideas, her beliefs on. We must learn from our mistakes, not repeat them. We have the answers, we just need to recognise them. It will not be easy, but we need to start our preparations now before it is too late. If we are to survive then we must return to Earth.

Like Christine's, mine is a hazardous journey, one that has already cost me a great deal. But, like her, I know I speak the truth and the truth is always worth the sacrifice.

THE CABAL

A.J Kirby is the award-winning published author of two novels and over forty short stories. He is a sportswriter for the Professional Footballer's Association and a reviewer for *The New York Journal of Books* and *The Short Review.*

Jacqueline Houghton writes character-led literary novels with fantasy/science fiction elements. She also works part-time as a geologist at the University of Leeds and has three children.

Jodie Daber is a twenty-something year old part-time secretary at the Arts Council. She lives in the North of England and her work, characterised by gothic flourishes and dark humour, has appeared in *Sein und Werden.*

Rachel Kendall is a thirty-five year old writer and editor living in Salford with her partner of photographic things and her daughter of much-messiness. The house is full of junk, dead curiosities (some stuffed, others skeletal), books, a toy tea-set, an Iggle Piggle, a few cameras, many films, stacking cups, a couple of stairgates and a clanger. She collects animal-feet brooches and loves the printed word. In 2009 her critically-acclaimed short story collection *The Bride Stripped Bare* was published by Dog Horn Publishing.

Richard Evans (born Manchester, United Kingdom, 1964), is author of the future-noir novel *Exilium* as well as two earlier books in the same series, *Machine Nation* and *Robophobia*. He was born in Manchester's Moss Side district. He has received several writing awards from Arts Council England and contributed robotics-related articles to UK publications, including *T3 Magazine* and the now-defunct *UFO Magazine*. The *T3 Magazine* article, 'Robosapiens', documents Richard's 2003 trip to CSAIL. He is currently writing a new novel, *Kosmonaut Zero*, due for publication in 2011.

I. SPIGEL DER KVNST VND NATVR.

ND - #0513 - 270225 - C0 - 234/156/12 - PB - 9781907133169 - Matt Lamination